THE CHALICE AND THE BLADE

JENNIFER LYNN

SOUL SONG PRESS, LLC

Published by Soul Song Press, LLC.

www.SoulSongPress.com

ISBN 978-0-9998434-1-3 (Paperback)

ISBN 978-0-9998434-2-0 (E-book)

For the Goddess, the God and the Creator...
with deepest gratitude.

AUTHOR'S NOTE

Welcome to *The Chalice and the Blade* !

Throughout Bree MacLeod's story, you will encounter words, phrases and concepts from the Celtic mystical and shamanic traditions. To preserve their integrity and authenticity, these ideas are presented in their source language, Gaelic.

No doubt many of you may be unfamiliar with this ancient tongue. No worries. To help you identify any such words and more easily connect with their magic and mystery, Gaelic words (both Irish and Scots) appear in italics throughout the story. While explanations are provided both through the narrative and context, a more complete glossary of these terms is included at the back of this book. Beyond the glossary is a list of references and resources, for those inspired to seek the Truth at the root of Bree's fiction.

May the light of *Imbas* ever flame the fire in your head.

Beannachtaí... Blessings.

Jennifer Lynn

1

Bree MacLeod stared at the plush couch and loveseat snuggled against the shadows of the darkened living room. Gwen loved those chairs.

"They are so welcoming," Gwen had insisted. Bree bought them just to see that smile on her lover's face. Now they sat empty, silenced and waiting.

Bree blinked back tears.

Eighteen months. She last saw those chairs from the open doorway of their University Hills apartment. Switching off the light, Bree had cast her eyes through the room one last time. Then, without a word, she locked the door behind her and flew to Ireland with no plans to return.

Nothing has changed.

Turning to her right, she leaned upon the wooden surface of the round, three-person dining table. Their table.

Tears welled again and threatened to spill down her cheeks. Widening her eyes, Bree slid into her usual seat at the table. Sleep-tossed, black hair fell across her face. She shoved the coarse strands aside and shifted her gaze down the foyer to her left. She could just see it, her still-packed suitcase, waiting by the closed front door.

Arriving far later than planned, she had dropped it there last night before wrapping herself in the fleece throw blanket at the foot of their bed and falling asleep.

Everything I need is in there. She eyed the soft-sided travel case. *It would be so easy. Just pick it up, lock the door and slip away...*

"When you cannot go around," the voice of her Salmon Ally called from the Otherworld, *"you must go through."*

Bree frowned. Salmon was correct. She knew it well enough. She had been running for more than a year, hiding in the thatched cottage in Kildare, Ireland, she inherited upon her mother's death. But sorrow had found her there, too.

She closed her eyes and tears spilled down her cheeks. As her body rocked with the release, she let the tears fall.

Bree balled her hands into fists. She was so tired of crying. She had marked the past year with weeping—every fire festival, each turning of the moon.

Fighting the cascade, Bree slowed her breathing. Consciously, she inhaled through her nose and exhaled through her mouth. As her body matched the rhythm of her breath, her training engaged.

Then the world around her blurred, the chair beneath her dissolved and she fell into the Otherworld...

...Thick, cold moss pulls at bare feet as Bree runs through a darkened forest. All around her shouts ricochet through the gloom. Tree limbs throw deepening shadows and she struggles to breathe the dense, stifling air.

Heavy footsteps shake the earth behind her and Bree spins on her heel. Tilting off-balance, she loses her footing in the soft undergrowth.

Darkness swallows her.

Bree stands frozen, her heart pounding. Groping blindly, she stretches her hands before her and something cold grazes her fingertips.

A woman screams. The sound slices through Bree and she falls. Her shoulder rocks against something hard and her breath rushes out in a grunt. As she gasps for breath, fire blazes to life before her. In a crimson-orange flash, it consumes the forest to encircle her.

Heart pounding, Bree pushes herself to her knees and rises carefully to her feet. All around her, fire snaps and hisses. Hungry, crimson-orange tongues lick at her, lashing closer and closer...

Bree opened her eyes. Fighting to slow her racing breath, she found herself held in a gentle, loving gaze. The goddess Bríghid, Bree's Otherworldly Teacher and the mother of her lineage, watched her from the opposite chair.

"No more running."

Bríghid's voice—feminine, ancient, loving—reverberated through Bree as a soft thud sounded from the oakwood floor beneath her. Bree glanced toward her feet. Just to the left of her bare toes rested a stone carving of a fleur-de-lys.

Bree inhaled sharply. She knew that stone. She saw it last in a journey, during her recent stay on the Isle of Skye, Scotland. A gift from her Otherworldly Allies, the stone was the reason she had returned to St. Louis.

Lifting her gaze, she looked into the eyes of her Teacher.

Mother Bríghid shook her head. *"No more running, Bree Nic Bhríde."*

Bree bristled at the sound of her Gaelic name. That was new, too. Another remnant of her stay on the Isle of Skye.

She bent down and picked up the stone. Gentle warmth flooded through her palm and pooled in the tips of her fingers. As she raised it closer to her face, her hand pulsated, reverberating like a heartbeat.

Her hazel eyes drifting across the image, she considered the stone. Small enough to tuck into the palm of her hand, it was ornately carved and deceptively heavy.

In her inner vision, a small fracture cracked the heart of the central petal. Tiny fissures stretched from the opening as a crimson-colored liquid welled to the surface. Her hand trembling, Bree watched the viscous fluid creep toward the edges of the fleur-de-lys. She blinked. Blood trickled from the stone and spilled to the floor.

2

A knock sounded at the door.

Bree looked up to find the seat opposite her empty. Mother Bríghid was gone. Beyond the wooden dining table, the couch and loveseat still snuggled under the shadows in the living room and her suitcase, packed and ready, waited by the door.

Gentle warmth pulsed through her hand and Bree lowered her gaze. The stone fleur-de-lys rested quietly in her palm. No blood spilled from it now. As another knock reverberated through the room, Bree closed her fingers around the stone and rose from the table.

She walked toward the front door, bare feet padding quietly upon the oakwood floor. As the foyer enfolded her, the sound of Gwen's laughter echoed through her and pulled Bree into memory. Knocking had summoned Bree to the door then, too. But before she could reach it, the door had opened and Gwen's smiling face peeked through the opening. A single key dangled on a fleur-de-lys chain in front of her lover.

"Sorry," she had shrugged, grinning madly. "Forgot you gave me a key."

The ghostly image of Gwen walked through the doorway into the darkened apartment and Bree opened shaking arms to embrace her lover. With a smile, Gwen stepped toward her and disappeared.

Bree stood alone in the foyer. Arms sinking to her sides, she stared at the unopened door. Silently, knowing better, she willed it to open.

She dropped her gaze and shook her head. *Gwen will never open that door again.*

Another knock sounded.

"Bree?" Warm and resonant, the familiar voice of Fergus Sinclair drifted through the door.

Bree's shoulders slumped and she stared at the oakwood floor.

Am I really ready for this?

"*When you cannot go around,*" the voice of her Salmon Ally called from the Otherworld, "*you must go through.*"

Fergus Sinclair was one of Bree's closest friends. She met him several years ago at an otherwise forgettable medical conference. A rather smug colleague had introduced him as "the other alternative practitioner in the room." Bree shook her head, remembering. The man intended to be rude, but Bree could only be grateful. Fergus was kind, supportive and encouraging, and he always offered a laugh when she needed it most.

Bree glanced into the darkened living room. In a flash, she saw it all again. Gwen's laughing eyes rounding in surprise... her lover falling, crumpling to the floor... Bree's hands outstretched, reaching, empty.

She lifted her gaze to the couch. Fergus had been there for her then, too. He came to the hospital just to drive Bree home. But when they arrived at her apartment, he stayed. All through that terrible night he sat with her on the couch, rocking her in his arms as she mumbled over and over, "DOA."

Bree closed her eyes.

After Gwen's death, Bree slowly fell to pieces. That couch became her world. Without being asked, Fergus had looked after her. He brought food and shared his meals with her, making sure she ate at least twice a day. Other times, he dropped by just to babble cheerfully to her about the day's events. When Bree could not tolerate idle chatter, he sat beside her in silence.

On more than one occasion, Fergus even dragged her off the couch and walked her to her favorite park. He understood her connection to the land and her love affair with the oak trees. He had even driven Bree to the airport when the pain of life in St. Louis without Gwen became too much.

Bree opened her eyes. Exhaling slowly, she stared at the closed front door of her apartment.

"Say hello to your boyfriend for me." Gwen's voice whispered beside Bree.

Gwen was always teasing Bree about their relationship, but Bree had never taken her seriously. Beyond a few curious kisses, Bree had never been drawn to men. She could appreciate their fierce beauty, even enjoy a harmless moment of flirtation, but a man had never held her interest beyond the trifling.

Until Scotland.

Deep brown eyes flashed in her inner vision as dark curls danced in a breeze. Heat prickled her skin and Bree frowned. *Not that that went anywhere.* Despite the mutual attraction, her brief interlude with Hamish MacSween had ended before it began.

The soft chime of a Tibetan singing bowl spilled through the foyer as the telephone in her jeans' pocket vibrated. Pulling it out, she read the text from Fergus.

"Are you awake?"

"He loves you," Gwen whispered beside Bree. *"Answer it. Answer it, with my blessing."*

Bree gazed at the closed door. In her mind's eye, her Salmon Ally hovered there, watching, waiting.

Okay, Salmon.

She shoved her telephone back into her pocket and called through a raspy throat. "Coming."

3

Bree pulled open the door to her apartment. Where familiar fiery red hair and hazel eyes should have greeted her, a brown paper bag hovered in mid-air. Bree's eyes flowed along the curling symbol of the fleur-de-lys printed across its surface to the words Café de Lys.

Fergus Sinclair lowered the bag just far enough for his eyes to meet Bree's. "I thought you might be hungry."

The stone in her hand burned. Bree shifted it into the pocket of her jeans. "What's in the bag?"

Fergus chuckled, his red hair spilling loose down broad shoulders. "Your favorite, of course."

Bree crooked an eyebrow. "Sheila's bison burger?"

"And a bear claw."

A smile spread across Bree's face. She reached for the bag and her hand brushed his. Shivering slightly, she pulled the door wide and stepped to the side before offering her friend a bow.

"Then, well met and enter in Peace."

Bree pushed the door closed behind him and padded barefoot down the hall. Heading for the dining table, she ducked under a broad shoulder and side-stepped around his lean torso.

Fergus chuckled behind her. "Welcome home."

Bree set the bag on the table. Pulling it open, she peeked inside, then looked up at her friend. "Nothing for you?"

Fergus shook his head. "I ate my lunch at the clinic." He lifted the paper take-out tray in his left hand and Bree spotted two Café de Lys paper cups. "So, I opted for coffee."

Bree narrowed her eyes at the tray. "Is one of those for me?"

A smile spreading across his face, Fergus pointed to the cup nearest Bree. "Americano, black, like rich soil."

Bree stepped close enough to lift the cup from the paper tray. Glancing at him, she nodded. "Good man." She raised the cup to her nose and, closing her eyes, inhaled deeply.

Nectar of the gods.

"*Sláinte, mo chairde...*" She opened her eyes to see Fergus' cup hovering between them. "Cheers, my friend."

She touched her cup to his. "*Sláinte.*"

Bree took a sip and swallowed. Delightful, nutty warmth poured through her as she peered through slitted eyes. "That woman pulls good coffee."

Fergus took another swallow from his cup. "That she does." He tilted his head toward the open bag on the table. "Please eat, before it gets cold."

Bree settled into her chair and pulled the take-out containers from the bag. She hardly noticed as Fergus placed his coffee cup on the table, then picked up the empty bag and dropped the tray into it. Before unwrapping her burger, she turned briefly to see him disappear down the hall into the kitchen.

She bit into the bison burger. Bacon-imbued juice slid down her throat as she chewed. Swallowing, she sighed and took another bite.

Fergus slipped into the chair opposite her and sipped his coffee. "Good?"

"Mmmmm.... Mmmmmm... Mmmmmm."

Bite after delicious bite, Bree devoured the burger. Then she lifted her cup of coffee, leaned back in her chair and closed her eyes.

Great Goddess, blessed is Your bounty. Thank You.

Bree opened her eyes.

"Better?"

"Getting there."

Fergus' gaze drifted to the darkened living room. She saw his eyes scan the empty couch and loveseat in the corner, then hover on the window shades, drawn to hold back the noontime sun. Slowly, he shifted in his seat to face her.

"Are you settling in okay?"

Bree's eyes darted to her still-packed suitcase by the door. From the corner of her eyes she noticed Fergus' head turn and track her line of sight. His quiet sigh rippled across her and she shivered. She dropped her gaze to the cup of coffee between her hands. Wrapping them more tightly around it, she focused on the warmth seeping into her as she shrugged.

Fergus cleared his throat. "Do you have plans for the afternoon?"

"Are you planning to unpack?" The unspoken question ached through Bree. She hugged the coffee cup in her hands. *Not yet.*

Slowly, her eyes rooted to the cup, she nodded. "I thought I would stop by the café."

With an exhale, she lifted her gaze to meet Fergus'. He leaned forward, resting an arm on the table. "I'm sure Sheila has the place in hand."

Bree leaned back in her chair. "It's Tuesday. Tasha will be in the office."

"Couldn't that wait a day or two?"

She shook her head. "It's been over a year since we reviewed accounts. I am sure she has kept it all up to date, but..." Bree sighed heavily. "Gwen left the café to me. I owe it to her to make sure it thrives."

His hazel eyes watched her in silence.

"He loves you," Gwen whispered from the seat next to Bree.

Fergus had never said as much, but Bree knew it was true. The thought sent heat pulsing through her and she scowled.

Coffee cup in hand, Fergus stood. "Well, the girls will be happy to see you."

Bree trailed behind Fergus as he started toward the door.

Reaching for the doorknob, he let his hand fall and turned back to face her.

"I finish with patients at six tonight. How about I pick you up afterward for dinner? Any place you like. Consider it a welcome home treat."

Bree gestured toward the empty take-out containers on the table. "I thought that's what this was."

"Nah. That's just good friends looking after each other." Fergus leaned his head toward hers, his eyes searching hers. "I'll text you when I'm leaving the clinic?"

She shrugged. "Okay."

"Good."

Fergus pulled the door open with his free hand and stepped into the doorway. "By the way, Sheila has really missed you."

Bree watched the front door close behind him. As she stood listening to his footsteps disappear down the walkway, her eyes settled again upon her packed suitcase.

"Anytime you are ready," it whispered.

4

Bree steered her Jeep Wrangler along the winding drive of the Sophia Center. The ancient trees shadowing the lane waved long, leafy limbs in greeting as she passed. Slowing, she followed the final curve into the parking lot behind the center and pulled the truck into her usual parking space.

The willow tree before her swayed. *"Welcome back,"* it whispered.

She stared at the weeping limbs of the tree. Shifting into park, she cut the engine and sat back in her seat. She had not intended to come here today. She left University City heading for a quiet spot along the Missouri River. She had planned to say a proper hello to the local land and water spirits before continuing on to the Café de Lys. She did not realize she had been rerouted until she turned onto the gravel entrance road to the Center.

Clearly her Allies had plans of their own.

I shouldn't be here.

Turning her head to the right, she gazed across the well-tended woodland. In the distance, small, pink blossoms dotted her favorite ring of apple trees.

Should be a good harvest.

"Pick some for me this season." Gwen's ghostly image smiled at Bree

from the passenger seat. *"You know how much I love those apples. So crisp and juicy. Nothing better."*

Tears welled in Bree's eyes.

"I remember the first time you brought me here." Gwen rambled beside her. *"We'd been together about a year, wasn't it?"*

Tears spilled down Bree's cheeks. Nodding mutely, she cast her gaze deeper into the woodland.

"You said you wanted to go for a walk." Gwen's soft chuckle washed over her as Bree's eyes spotted the familiar, wooden archway. *"Wasn't quite what I imagined."*

Bree stiffened in her seat. Turning away from her dead lover, she opened the door and pushed out of the Jeep. A few quick strides carried her across the gravel parking area to the edge of the park itself. As her feet touched the grassy earth of the woodland, she froze. Her body trembled. She could not take another step.

The wooden archway caught her gaze. Bree knew what waited beyond that woven trellis. Countless hours she had spent in that sacred circle, held in the loving refuge of the stones and the trees. She had walked that labyrinth to its center every fire festival on the Great Wheel of Life since she moved to St. Louis. Winding with its pathway to the very core of her soul, she always discovered the thing she could not see on her own. And—every time—the Lady of the Labyrinth had sheltered her, whispered to her the Truth needed to set her soul flame ablaze.

What would She whisper to me today? Bree dropped her gaze to the square toes of her boots. *Do I even want to hear it?*

Bree's shoulders slumped. *I shouldn't be here.*

She pivoted back toward the truck and stopped short. She stood face to face with her dead mother, Bríde.

"You cannot run from this." Bríde shook her head. *"Not you."*

Bree stared into her mother's pleading eyes.

"Remember who you are."

"I cannot, not today." Bree stepped to the side. Her mother remained in front of her.

"You must, Bree. Your very blood demands it. Or have you forgotten?"

Bree dropped her gaze to the earth beneath her and closed her eyes. Fiery, blue light flashed through her inner vision. One after another, women's names etched themselves before her, their connections branching across eons in opalescent trees. Brí, Bríanna, Bríseanna, Bríghlín, Brígh... Blazing against the darkness of her inner vision, they tracked the generations of her Irish lineage.

Forgotten? Hardly. Bree knew these names. Time and again she had seen them, read them, heard them whispered from the Otherworld. She suspected they were inscribed upon her very soul.

"Must I remind you, Bree? You are a Bean feasa, a wise woman, a shaman. One of the Aes Dána, the Gifted. The blood that runs in your veins is the blood of Bríghid, the Celtic goddess of the Sacred Flame. Just as Her blood gifts you, it calls your soul to the Work.

"As it did for me and those before us, Her Gift empowers you to see and move through the Veil between the world of physical reality and the world of soul. Once accepted, that Gift becomes a mandate. You can try to ignore it, Bree. But as a first-born daughter of Bríghid, you carry the fullness of this Gift and must answer the call."

"Not today."

Bree moved another step to the side. Still, her mother remained in front of her.

"Every day."

Bree matched her mother's resolute gaze. "I thought it was always my choice?"

"It is. And you made this choice when you entered the grove and embraced your initiation. You are committed. That promise holds you, now and throughout this lifetime."

Bree looked over her shoulder at the wooden archway behind her.

"Stop running from who you are."

Bree shut her eyes. "You don't understand. I formally released my connection to this place over a year ago, before I left for Ireland." She shook her head as she gestured to the woodland behind her. "Mother, can you honestly say it would be wise to casually reopen what was properly and intentionally closed?"

She waited in silence. Opening her eyes, she lifted her face to her mother. But, she was alone. Only the parking area stretched before her.

With a sigh, Bree started back toward her Jeep. Gravel crunched beneath her boots as she crossed the parking area and pulled open the door. Removing the car key from her pocket, she slid into the driver's seat.

"*So,*" Gwen's voice drifted from the passenger seat. "*I take it, that's a no for walking today?*"

5

As the door drifted closed behind her, Bree took three steps into the Café de Lys and stopped. Sunlight streamed through the floor-to-ceiling windows, flooding the café and bathing the guests sitting on the overstuffed sofas in soft, golden light. Faery light, Gwen used to call it, her own kiss of magic.

"Bree!" A woman squealed from behind the espresso machine, then launched herself over the counter. Arms flailing above curly, red hair, she ran across the room. "Bree! Breeeeeee!"

Nodding slowly, Bree gestured to the woman. "Hello, Sheila." Then she cast her gaze around the open room and sighed.

I'm really here.

"Bree!"

"Oooooof!" Bree turned toward Sheila's voice and found herself lifted into a bear hug. Her toes just reaching the floor, she struggled to keep her balance.

As Bree's feet settled onto wood again, Sheila stepped back and propped her hands on her hips. "Fergus said you'd be coming." She chuckled and shook her head. "Serves me right for not believing him. I thought he was teasing me, again."

"She's so quick to laugh, that one." Gwen's voice echoed through Bree. Dropping her gaze to the left, a ghostly image of her former lover flickered in the sunlight, standing beside her. Just like she always did. The ghostly woman smiled at Bree. *"And she's so easy to tease."*

Bree blinked back tears as a gentle warmth spread up her legs and torso.

"You look well enough." Sheila's gaze softened, bathing Bree in tender compassion. "Glad you're back with us."

Bree lifted her eyes to meet the woman's and offered her a thin smile. *Am I?*

Red eyebrows darted upward. "The usual?"

"Sure," Bree shrugged.

"Right!" Sheila clapped her hands together and rubbed them. "Coming right up!"

Bree watched Gwen's favorite barista stride back toward the coffee bar. *She and Gwen, they always loved this place.* Bree sighed and looked around the room. Soft, golden sunlight spilled from the windows, illuminating her favorite loveseat. She walked up to the overstuffed chair, reached out and ran her fingers along the ribbing on the lavender throw pillows.

"You must help me."

Bree lifted her gaze toward the woman's voice. Oak trees stretched all around her, their autumn leaves spilling a sea of orange and red through the old-growth forest. Her breath clouded before her, lingering on the damp, chilly air, and she shivered. She turned to look for the woman who had summoned her here.

"You must help me."

Turning toward the frantic voice, Bree hit something solid. Fire seared across her arm.

"Oh, Bree!" Sheila cried out and took a step back. "I'm so sorry!"

A cloth napkin pressed against her arm as Sheila cleaned the spilled coffee from her skin. In Bree's inner vision, blood seeped from the reddened cloth and dripped onto the floor at her feet.

"Are you okay?"

Bree lifted her gaze. Before her, a ceramic chalice curved in Sheila's hands. Etched in spiraling chevrons, the ancient vessel radiated opalescent light.

"Bree?"

Sheila touched her arm and Bree's gaze snapped to meet the woman's. When she looked back at Sheila's hands, they held an ordinary cup of coffee. Bree frowned.

"Here," Sheila's voice flowed soft, echoing Gwen's tone and words, as she encouraged Bree into the overstuffed chair. "Have a seat. Just relax and let me care for you for a while."

Shaking slightly, Bree sank into the soft cushions. To her left, Sheila leaned forward and placed what remained of the cup of coffee on the low table before Bree.

"Is Tasha in the office?"

Sheila turned and studied Bree's face. The look of caring concern made Bree wonder just what, or how much, Sheila saw.

"Of course. Want me to tell her you're here?"

Bree nodded mutely.

Sheila cast a long glance in Bree's direction, then turned and disappeared into the back.

Bree stared at the coffee cup. Now perfectly ordinary, steam rose from the rich, dark liquid within it to dissolve into the sunlight streaming in through the floor-to-ceiling windows of the café.

She shook her head. "What's that all about?"

The bouncing notes of an Irish jig poured around her as the telephone in her jeans' pocket vibrated. Pulling it out, Fergus' number glowed on the screen. She pressed answer and lifted the telephone to her ear.

"Changed your mind so soon?"

"What?" The soft haze of puzzlement drifted over her. "No, dinner is definitely a go." Fergus paused. "I was calling with a professional question."

Bree's eyebrows rose. "Which is?"

"I know you're only just home, but..." Fergus' voice wavered. "Are you available for work?"

Light flashed before Bree and pooled to bathe her coffee cup in a golden halo. As Bree stared, the cup grew a long stem and the basin rounded to form a chalice. Weeping through the ceramic sides, blood slid down to the base and spilled onto the floor at her feet.

"Yes," Bree exhaled. "Yes, I am."

6

"Bree? Is that really you?"

Bree's head snapped toward the resonant voice and grey-blue eyes flashed with a smile. Telephone still at her ear, Bree waved with her free hand.

Thick, dark braids stretched, eager to escape the elastic band atop the heart-shaped face, as Tasha grimaced. Brilliant eyes widening, she covered her generous mouth with both hands.

"It's okay," Bree whispered. Offering a smile of her own, she patted the cushion of the chair to her left.

"Is someone there?" Fergus' voice drew Bree back to the telephone.

"Tasha just walked up."

"Ah." A stream of prickles ran up Bree's spine as Fergus cleared his throat. "How about I tell you the details over dinner then?"

Bree considered the weeping chalice before her. "Can it wait that long?"

"It can." Fergus hesitated. "But, if I may, I will let the patient know you are available."

Bree sat back in her chair. "Agreed."

"Excellent. See you around six."

The call disconnected and Bree leaned forward to place her telephone on the table before her. The chalice and the blood were gone. Once again steam drifted skyward out of an ordinary, Café-de-Lys coffee cup. Then golden light blazed, etching the curling imprint of the fleur-de-lys.

Bree's fingers shook as she reached to trace the image. *I'm coming.*

"Bree?"

She turned to face Tasha and shook her head. "Sorry," she offered before settling back again in her chair.

Gleaming eyes bathed Bree in gentle concern as they drifted across her face. "You okay? Sheila said you seemed a bit... unsteady."

"Just tired." Bree offered her friend a wan smile. "I'm still on Irish time."

Tasha's eyes narrowed, studying her.

"There She is again," Gwen chuckled beside her.

Bree dropped her gaze to her square-toed boots.

"Seriously," Gwen teased from the chair beside Bree. *"Don't tell me you still can't see Her."* Sunlight spilled through her dead lover as she leaned forward to gesture toward their friend. *"Flowing white toga. Owl perched on Her arm. She is Athena, clear as day."*

Bree could still remember when Tasha first walked into the café, white dress spilling down bare shoulders and sumptuous curves. It was the only time in their years together Bree remembered hearing Gwen stammer. "It's... you're... the job is yours."

After a dazzling smile and firm handshake, Gwen had stood gaping as she watched Tasha walk out the door. "Athena. The goddess Athena. In my café."

"I know. I know." Bree's dead lover rolled her eyes beside her. *"Daughter of Athena."*

Bree shook her head and sighed. "And, I suppose," she tilted her face back to Tasha, "it is strange to be here."

Tasha leaned forward. "I didn't think you'd be back."

"Honestly," Bree blinked. "I wasn't sure I would be."

Tasha nodded. In Bree's inner vision, an image of her still-packed suitcase wavered. *"Any time you are ready."*

"Well," Tasha smiled, her grey-blue eyes shimmering, "it's good to see you. As always."

Sheila rounded Tasha's chair, a plate balanced in her right hand. Bending forward, she placed it on the table directly before Bree. "Turkey croissant with onions, lettuce and mayo. Just the way you like it." With a wink, she straightened and, humming softly, headed back toward the espresso bar.

Bree watched her walk away, then stared at the unrequested sandwich.

From the chair beside her, Tasha chuckled softly, her braids spilling as she shook her head. "That girl's got a soft spot for you."

7

"I had a good chat with Tasha today." Bree lifted her glass of water and took a sip. "Seems everything is going well at the café. Better than ever, actually."

Fergus sat opposite her in the wooden booth of the Gráinne Uaile, her favorite pub in St. Louis' Central West End. "Better than ever," Fergus rested his arms on the wooden table. "That's good, right?"

"More than good. It's a relief."

"Why do you say that?"

"Because," she leaned back against the high backrest of the wooden booth, "that means the café can thrive without me."

Fergus nodded. "The café was Gwen's passion, not yours."

"It still is." Bree shifted in her seat and shrugged. "I am happy for it to keep going..."

"As long as you don't have to run it."

Bree smiled. "Exactly."

Her gaze drifted across the room and Bree exhaled a soft sigh. She had missed this place.

Framed newspaper articles and mementos from the owner's

travels to Ireland dotted the plain brick walls. She had been dining there for years, yet during every visit she discovered something new.

She glanced at the wall to her left. There, nestled between a map of the clan names of Ireland and a County Mayo hurling jersey, hung a local artist's imagining of the gastropub's namesake, Gráinne Ní Mháille. Bree paused to consider the far-seeing eyes and commanding stance the artist imparted to the sixteenth-century pirate queen of County Mayo, Ireland.

She smiled up at the image. A Clew Bay woman, Gráinne Uaile's actions broke all the conventions of the day. Despite having an older brother, she stepped into her father's leadership upon his death and became the mistress of the seas. When her sons and husband were captured by the English, she sailed to London. There, she petitioned the crown for an audience with Queen Elizabeth I and won not only a hearing but freedom for her loved ones.

A wild, Fenian cailín to the core.

Bree raised her glass of water and saluted the long-dead woman. Somehow, she was certain—she and the wild woman of the western seas would have been good friends.

"You must help me."

Bree's breath caught in her throat. Inhaling slowly, she lowered her glass toward the table and let it slide between her fingers the last few inches to the surface. Her eyes darted furtively, scanning the large room. Dark, wooden tables and chairs waited patiently for new arrivals while current guests chatted and shared laughter along with their meals. Pictures and posters covered the walls, singing the story of Ireland. Wait staff gossiped in the corner.

Bree exhaled.

Fergus reached a hand toward hers, then pulled it back as the waitress arrived and slid a heaping basket of homemade potato crisps onto the table between them.

"Here you go," the woman smiled at Bree. "Chips, no rarebit."

"Thanks, Chelle." Bree returned the smile, admiring the woman's newly cropped and red-tipped, brown hair. "You are so good to me."

"Nothing easier, hon." Chelle winked. "The rest will be up soon. Enjoy."

Soft and tender, rosy-pink light shimmered through Bree. Drinking it in, she let the world drift away. Fergus, Gráinne Uaile and the Otherworldly voice—she let it all go as she watched Chelle's swaying form disappear through the wooden archway into the other room.

Warmth spread through her right hand. Shifting her gaze, she discovered Fergus' hand resting on hers. She lifted her gaze to meet his.

"You okay?"

Bree shivered and pulled her hand out from under his. "Sure." She dropped her hands to the bench beneath her and pressed herself against the wooden backrest of the booth. *Just breathe.* "Tell me about the Work you mentioned this afternoon."

Fergus' hand lingered on the table, then reached for a chip. "It's for a patient of mine."

He popped the chip into his mouth and Bree waited in silence as he chewed. He had consulted her before on patient care, but she could count on one hand the number of times he had asked her to actively get involved. Like Bree, Fergus took his responsibilities as a healer very seriously.

Fergus shook his head. "It's the strangest thing. She came to see me because she was hemorrhaging. Her menstrual cycle was flooding endlessly. Her gynecologist performed a D&C, but she just kept on bleeding.

"I had treated her sister's irregular menstrual cycle, which is how Pamela—that's the patient's name—found me. She was terribly weak even then. When we were able to stop the blood loss, I thought she would grow stronger again." He heaved a sigh. "She hasn't. In fact, she's getting weaker."

Fergus stared at his water glass, his eyebrows slowly furrowing. "It's like her life force is just draining away." He glanced up at Bree. "I've been treating her with a combination of moxa and acupuncture. I also send her home with a rectifying and nourishing Chinese herbal formula focused on clearing wasting heat and banking the Zheng qi. She improves slightly—for a couple days, maybe a week—then she begins wasting again.

"Her pulses have improved, some. Overall, however, they slowly continue to weaken. I've even shifted her to treatment twice a week. That's why I suggested she consult her gynecologist for re-evaluation." Fergus stared at Bree. "Nothing. She has seen her GYN, her GP, a hematologist, an oncologist, even an infectious disease specialist. Their tests all say nothing is wrong with her."

"Let me guess," Bree swallowed the chip she was chewing. "They have referred her to a psychiatrist."

"She is *not* crazy, Bree."

"I know." Bree offered her friend a consoling smile.

Fergus leaned forward. "Her sister came in to see me today. I didn't ask about Pamela. As if confidentiality issues weren't enough of a consideration, I don't like to muddy the waters of a session by bringing in other people's energies. You know that."

Bree nodded.

"Her sister told me—Pamela started bleeding again."

"You must help me."

Light flashed, drawing Bree's gaze back to her water glass. The clear basin rounded before her eyes and a thin shoot pressed out from its base. While the goblet rose on the lengthening stem, the glass darkened, concealing the liquid within it. Bree watched the vessel grow thicker and roughen into the ceramic chalice she had seen earlier that afternoon. As opalescent light etched spiraling chevrons across its surface, blood wept through the sides and spilled onto the wooden table.

Eyes fixed on the pooling blood, Bree exhaled. "Tell her I will see her tomorrow."

8

Pulling the key out of the lock, Bree pushed open the front door of her apartment. Shadows swayed and swirled before her as a ray of moonlight trickled into the darkened foyer.

She reached inside and snapped on the hall light. Her still-packed suitcase sat just to the left, waiting for her. She stepped into the vestibule and stood staring at the black, soft-sided bag as the door fell closed behind her.

"Long day?"

Bree looked up into Gwen's smiling face. Soul light flickering, her dead lover stood in the foyer's entrance.

"I would have cooked dinner for you, but..." Gwen shrugged. As her arms dropped to her sides, her red curls tossed against her head.

"That's okay. I already ate." Bree slipped out of her boots and placed them next to her suitcase.

"What did Sheila make for you this time?"

Bree shook her head. "She didn't. I ate dinner at the pub, with Fergus."

"Oh?"

Bree cringed. She knew that tone. Playful on the surface, but deadly at the core. Clearly, her lover had something on her mind.

"It wasn't like that."

Gwen stood staring at her, a blank look pasted on her face.

The hairs on the back of Bree's neck stood on edge. *Be careful*, she reminded herself.

Bree did not know just what her dead lover was up to, but she was certain this conversation would end badly. It always did when Gwen feigned indifference. And the last thing Bree wanted right now was a fight.

Bree stepped around the ghostly image of her lover and headed down the hallway to her right.

Her socks slipping on the oakwood floor, she continued past the kitchen and the guest bedroom which Gwen always called their library. Bree had to admit, it housed books far more regularly than anything, or anyone, else.

As she approached the end of the hallway, the open door to her left pulled at her. Slowing her pace, she let her eyes linger upon the spiraling lines of the tricele she herself had painted on the wood.

For a heartbeat, she hesitated, then shook her head. *Not tonight.* Instead, she turned to the right and walked into their bedroom.

Reaching around the door jamb, she flipped on the light. Legs crossed, Gwen sat perched on her side of the bed.

Without a word, Bree crossed to her own side of the room and slipped out of her jeans and black dragon tee shirt. Tossing the dirty clothes into the hamper just inside the closet, she stepped in front of her dresser and pulled open the second drawer from the bottom. She grabbed the shirt on top and pulled it over her head before pushing the drawer closed.

She stretched her arm just far enough to flip off the light, then let her feet carry her to the bed. Yawning noisily, she reached for the edge of the quilt and froze. Her hand hovered a few inches above the familiar, sage green comforter.

"It won't bite you."

Bree's eyes met those of her dead lover. Gwen was right. Bree knew it. Still, she could not bring herself to sleep under those covers.

With a sigh, Bree straightened and turned to her left. She reached, instead, for the tan, fleece throw blanket folded across the foot of their bed. Wrapping herself in it, she laid down and stared into the darkness.

"Just how long are you planning to haunt me, anyway?"

-

9

Bree stands in a forest. Trees dressed in their autumn splendor spread all around her as a sea of gold, orange and red leaves covers the thick moss at her feet. Her breath hangs heavy in the damp air. A cold breeze rustles the leaves and races across her back. Shivering, she pulls her woolen cloak more tightly around her shoulders.

Another gust sends her black hair streaming across her face and she draws the hood of the cloak up and over her head. Turning a slow circle, she lets her gaze drift through the surrounding forest. Her eyes search for a familiar branch or clustering of trees but find none.

"Where am I?" Her breath clumps as mist upon the cooling air.

Leaves snap and crackle behind her. Bree turns just as a woman crashes into her.

Struggling for balance, Bree grasps the woman by the shoulders in an effort to steady them both. A large bundle slips from the woman's arms and she teeters in Bree's hands as she lunges to recover it.

Bree sends her awareness running like roots into the earth beneath her. Drawing strength from the connection, she braces her legs. "Steady," she exhales. "I've got you."

The woman makes a strange sound, not quite a grunt but more than a whimper. Clasping the bundle to her belly, the woman hunches over it protectively and peers up at Bree. As the woman's dark eyes meet hers, terror pummels Bree.

Heat sears down her face and shoulders. Fire hissing in her ears, Bree watches the woman's gaze spill from her forehead and down the front of her cloak. In her mind's eye, Bree can see the spiraling symbols trimming the heavy wool flash with fiery, blue light. The ancient glyphs proclaim Bree both Healer and Initiate of the Mystery. She knows the woman can read them.

Dark eyes grip her. "You must help me."

"Who are you?"

Male voices shout in the distance, calling back and forth between groups. The woman tenses and trembles in Bree's hands. Again, terror races through her, all but strangling her. As the woman fights Bree's hold, Bree struggles to breathe.

"Hide," the woman's voice rasps. "I must find a place to hide."

Bree shakes her head. "We are deep in the forest, with only the trees for shelter."

The woman wrestles against Bree's hold, pulling one way and then another. Her eyes scan the forest floor and tree limbs around her. Frantic, she faces Bree and rams the bundle against Bree's belly.

Exhaling from the impact, Bree drops her hold on the woman and wraps her arms around the bundle. As she looks from the bundle to her companion, the woman shoves her backward. Bree's feet slip in the soft, damp undergrowth and she falls.

The forest floor rushes toward her and Bree tries to relax her back for the impact. But it never comes. Instead, she falls straight through the crust of the earth.

Deeper and deeper, she plummets, watching the earth race higher and higher above her. Dark, rich, loamy soil rises all around her, enfolds her, swallows her until, with a soft thud, she hits solid ground.

Clutching the woman's bundle to her belly, Bree rolls onto her side. She closes her eyes and struggles to catch her breath.

"Heh, heh, heh."

A deep, guttural chuckling greets her arrival. Still working to steady her breathing, Bree opens her eyes. Directly in front of her, mounds of pale earth rise, side by side.

Her eyes track up the smooth edges and she realizes each mound is as wide as Bree is tall! Then the hilltops suddenly flatten as a reedy, wood-like substance covers their softly sloping surfaces.

Bree frowns. Her eyes flow across the rolling expanse as she counts. "One... two... three..." She stretches her neck to follow the flowing mounds. "Four... five?"

"Wait," she squints her eyes. "Are those...?"

The mounds wiggle. She watches them rise and fall in rapid succession, waving from left to right, while the earth beneath her remains still.

"Toes." The word is a whisper on her lips. "Those are toes."

"Heh, heh, heh."

Bree sends her gaze running beyond the reed-like toenails, over a foot vast as a house to a giant-sized leg and the torso above it. Continuing past shoulders broad enough to span the Missouri river, she meets a familiar gaze.

Shifting the bundle into her left hand, Bree pushes herself up onto her right and bows her head.

The Dagda, the Great Father of the Celtic mystical tradition, stands before her. He shakes his massive head and chuckles.

Bree lifts her head. "What's so funny?"

The Dagda points to the bundle precariously balanced in Bree's left hand. Dropping her gaze, Bree scans the purple cloth in her arm.

Weight pulls at her, tugging her body closer to the ground. A leather strap stretches and crisscrosses the covering fabric. Squinting slightly, Bree strains for a better view of the ancient glyphs etched along the hide.

"Are those runes?"

The Dagda roars with laughter. Bree looks up to see his arms lengthen and coil under his belly to support his enormous, shaking stomach. Tiny shafts of light escape from the center of the jiggling belly and rush outward, streaming in endless spirals. As light and laughter blur together, they birth a sound Bree can only call screaming.

Cringing against the searing sound, darkness descends and swallows her.

10

Bree opened her eyes and sat bolt upright. Shadows stretched and hovered in the darkness surrounding her. She blinked, trying to restore her vision while her ears rang with a strange, distorted scream.

She reached up to cover her ears with her hands and something slid from her shoulders down to her waist. Redirecting her hands downward, she pressed into something soft. She grabbed hold of it and pulled it in front of her face. A fleece blanket came into view.

Bree turned the bit of blanket over and over in her hands. The screaming dissipated and her shoulders slackened, releasing a tension she had not realized was there. Looking around her, shapes emerged out of the darkness—a lamp, a closet door, a dresser. Her dresser.

It was a dream. I was journeying in a dream.

Tossing the blanket aside, she swung her legs over the edge of her bed and flipped on the nearest light. No trees appeared around her. Instead of moss and leaves, a familiar oakwood floor stretched under her bare feet. Grateful, Bree sighed.

The bouncing notes of an Irish jig rang out from her telephone. Out of habit, Bree reached toward the surface of her nightstand, only to find it empty. She glanced over to her dresser and pursed her lips. Her telephone was nowhere to be seen.

Bree tracked the sound to her closet and dug her jeans out of the hamper. As she tugged the ringing telephone out of her pocket, it slipped through her fingers and fell with a thud to the floor. She knelt down to search for it amongst the shadows. By the time she found it, the telephone had stopped ringing.

She stood up and peered at the message on the screen. *Missed call: Caitlìn MacLeod.*

Red-haired pig-tails spilled through her inner vision. For a heartbeat, Bree was a young girl again, running bare-footed upon endless sands. The brackish tang of salt water flooded through her nose and puckered her tongue. As girlish laughter echoed and deepened to the full throat of an adult, earth-colored eyes winked.

One year older than her, Caitlìn was one of Bree's oldest and dearest friends. Kinswomen, they shared the name MacLeod but no other direct, blood relationship. They met as young girls, growing up wild on the shores of Cape Breton.

After Bree's mother died, her father decided to leave Seattle and return with her to his hometown in Nova Scotia. But his grief proved too deep for him and Caitlìn's family welcomed Bree into their home. That made Bree and Caitlìn sisters, at least for the two years before Bree was sent to live with her mother's sister in Seattle.

Bree frowned at the glowing screen. *Why is Caitlìn calling?*

Over the years, Bree had remained close to Caitlìn and they always managed to find each other in times of transition or need. About three months ago Bree had stepped in to manage Heather House, her kinswoman's B&B on the Isle of Skye, Scotland, so Caitlìn could attend a funeral in Cape Breton. For a while, Bree even considered making Heather House her home. But, at the prompting of her Allies, she had returned to St. Louis.

Caitlìn's voice rose in Bree's memory. "Know this—ye have a place here any time ye have need or want of it."

Telephone in hand, Bree stepped out of the closet and sat on the edge of the bed. She stared at the screen. *If it's important, Caitlìn will leave a message.*

She waited. When no message activated her voicemail box, Bree tapped a finger on the comforter.

Should I call her back now?

She glanced at the clock on her screen. 2:05 am winked back at her. Adding six hours, Bree adjusted for Skye time. *Eight am.* She grimaced. She remembered all too well the early risings and hectic mornings at the inn, preparing breakfasts, cleaning the kitchen and checking guests out of Heather House.

But, she must be available. She just called me.

Bree swiped the missed call message on her telephone. As Caitlìn's number appeared on the screen, she pressed it. The tell-tale, European double ring sounded three times on the line before the soft brogue of Caitlìn's recorded voice greeted her.

"*Fàilte romhat* and welcome tae Heather House, your home across the waters..."

Bree waited for her chance to leave a message. Rubbing her eyes with her free hand, she yawned just as she heard the beep. "*Màidin mhaigh mo chairde...* Good morning, it's Bree. Saw you called. Am guessing you are elbow-deep in guest breakfasts right about now. Feel free to ring back when you can. Otherwise, I will call you this evening, Skye time."

She hung up and stared at the telephone in her hands. She sat waiting for it to ring, her eyes slowly drifting closed. When her head snapped upward with a start, she shook herself awake and checked for messages.

Nothing.

She frowned and ran her finger over the screen. Before her eyes, the telephone shut itself down into sleep mode. Staring at the darkened display, she decided sleep was an excellent idea.

I'll call her tomorrow.

She placed her telephone on her nightstand and switched off the light. Rolling herself back into the tan, fleece blanket, she closed her eyes. Two giant feet hovered in her mind's eye. The enormous toes wiggled, as if waving to her.

"The Dagda," she muttered. "What would the Dagda want with me?"

As she slid past consciousness into sleep, a deep, guttural chuckling echoed through her.

11

Bree steered her Jeep into a shady parking spot in front of the two-story, brick building. A converted, multi-family dwelling, the typical St. Louis structure now housed four local businesses, including the Chinese medicine clinic of Fergus Sinclair.

Bree turned off the engine and pulled the key out of the ignition. Reaching into the back seat, she grabbed the cloth bag containing her drum and shamanic essentials before hopping out of the truck. A few strides carried her up the short walkway and through the main entrance. Once inside, she skirted the stairs and headed for the door on the left.

Two dragons, one black and one white, chased each other's tails in a never-ending circle upon the glass surface of the door. As Bree reached out and grasped the handle, the black dragon to her left winked.

"Welcome back," the female voice whispered.

Returning the wink, Bree nodded.

A bell chimed its soft greeting above her head as she pushed open the door and stepped into the comfortable waiting room. Water gurgled in a small, ceramic fountain and the deep, earthy scent of moxa wrapped her in welcome. Bree had heard so many different descriptions of that nurturing aroma, from chocolate chip cookies baking to sage burning and even marijuana's after breath. None of them quite captured the unique, peaty fragrance of the mugwort root so ubiquitous to the practice of Chinese medicine. Bree had to admit, she could not offer a better description. She knew only, the scent always made her smile.

Bree closed her eyes and inhaled slowly. Gentle warmth spilled into her, flowing from her lungs outward to her fingertips, toes and head. A soft radiance rippled within that warmth, replenishing her.

Blessed is the Mother. Blessed is the Mystery.

Footsteps pattered upon the earth-colored carpet. Bree opened her eyes to see Fergus emerge from the room beyond. She glanced at his jeans and rust-colored, polo-style shirt and smiled. *Comfortable, as always.*

Fergus offered a smile in return. "Good morning."

"To you as well."

"Pamela isn't here yet. Kat, her sister, texted. Said they are running a few minutes late."

Bree nodded.

Fergus gestured to the open door behind him. "I set you up in there." Bree followed him to the doorway. "Do you need anything else?"

Bree peeked into the room before her. Sage-colored walls enfolded the same earth-colored carpet as the waiting room. Along the far wall, white rice-paper stretched within the black frame of a traditional shoji screen and a small curio cabinet displayed a glass jar of cotton balls, a red Sharps container and various boxes of acupuncture needles. Completing the transformation of the ordinary office space into a healing sanctuary, a wooden statue of Kwan Yin, the Eastern goddess of divine compassion and healing, extended open arms to everyone entering.

All that was missing was an acupuncture table. Bree knew that table had been carefully folded up and tucked away in preparation for today's session. In its place, purple, Zen-style meditation mats and cushions sat on either side of a low, wooden table adorned by a single, white candle in a crescent-shaped votive glass.

"No." She shook her head. "That should do it for now." She stepped just inside the treatment room and set down her drum bag. Leaning against the door jamb, she slid out of her boots.

"Bree." His hazel eyes held hers. "She is desperate."

Light flashed. Bree's breath rasped short and hard in her chest as her feet struggled to break free of the soft moss gripping them. All around her, male voices shouted in the distance. Darting wildly, her eyes scanned the forest floor for a path to freedom.

Leaves crunched to her right and she snapped her head toward the sound. The forest blurred out of view. She stood facing Fergus in the treatment room.

"I know."

12

The bell over the clinic's front door chimed its soft welcome. Fergus nodded to Bree. "Let me greet them first."

"Of course."

Bree watched Fergus disappear around the corner into the waiting room. Alone, she picked up her drum bag and walked over to the meditation cushions. Closing her eyes, she exhaled. With each breath, she let go—of the voices in the other room, of her own conflicting emotions, of the noise of life in St. Louis. Anything other than her own life force, she let it fall away. Exhaling deeply, she released it all back to the earth, back to the Mother, to the great Cauldron of Life.

Into the stillness, she whispered. "Show me north."

Engaging her inner vision, she pivoted carefully *deiseal*, turning sunwise in an ancient and physical prayer for life-affirming, co-creative flow. With each step, she sank into the deepening stillness and sent her awareness drifting through her body. Moving slowly, she watched, waited.

A touch, firm and distinct, pressed against her forehead. *There.* Opening her eyes, she noted the Kwan Yin statue stood, arms outstretched in welcome, on her right.

Bree smiled. *Of course he would place Her in the east. What better place for the goddess of healing than the direction of generosity, the rising sun and new beginnings?*

She looked at the meditation cushions. Fergus had placed one in the west and one in the east.

Perfect.

She stepped over to the cushion in the west. Sliding open the zipper, she pulled her favorite Walton's *bodhrán*, the one she used for client journeys, out of its cloth, carrier bag. A small woven pouch dangled from the two wooden slats crisscrossing the back and forming a handle for the drum. The small bag, she knew, contained a stone from a sacred well associated with the mother of her lineage, the goddess Bríghid, in the heart of Kildare, Ireland. Holding the drum in her left hand, Bree reached out and lifted the pouch to her lips.

Blessed is the Mother. Blessed is the Mystery. Sin é.

"Bree?"

Lowering her drum, she saw Fergus standing in the open doorway. A few steps behind him stood two women. One was fair-haired, the other dark, but the slant of the cheek bones and rounded lips declared them decidedly sisters.

Bree set her drum down on the meditation cushion in the west and offered the group a brief bow. "Come in," she gestured, "please."

Fergus stepped just inside the door and turned to face the two women. He nodded to the dark-haired sister. "Pamela, this is my colleague and friend, Bree MacLeod."

Dull, blue eyes stared into Bree's. She let her gaze drift across the surface of the woman's energy field and stifled a gasp. Where the light of the life force should shine and radiate outward, the energy field yielded, sunken and hollow. As Bree's vision adjusted to consider the frail body before her, the word *withered* rang through her mind.

"I'm Kat, Pamela's sister."

Force pushed so hard against Bree, she swayed in place. Shifting her stance to conceal the movement, she faced the blonde-haired woman. Worry pounded against Bree's awareness as Kat wrapped her arm around her sister. Pamela shrunk into her sister and, for a moment, Bree wondered if the woman would disappear in a blink.

"It's lovely to meet you both." She shifted her gaze to Pamela and smiled. "You are welcome to come in, if you still want to."

Pamela glanced at the meditation cushions and the candle on the table. Bree thought the woman withdrew even further behind the shield of her sister's energy field.

Fergus cleared his throat. "Pamela, would you like me to stay?"

The woman's blue eyes scanned the familiar shoji screen and curio cabinet. She shook her head. "That's okay, Fergus," the woman's voice was a whisper. "Kat will be with me."

Fergus extended his arms toward the frail woman. Carefully, folding her slight hand between his, he drew Pamela into the room. Following, her sister matched her, step for step.

He offered Pamela an encouraging smile. "If you change your mind..."

The dark-haired woman smiled thinly.

"Right," Fergus nodded. "Then I will leave you to it."

13

As Fergus pulled the door closed behind him, Bree gestured to the purple, meditation cushions on the floor.

"I thought these might be better for our session today. That way, if you feel like stretching out or napping while I journey, you can. But, if you would prefer a chair..."

"No." Pamela took an unsteady step toward the nearest cushion. "If Kat will help me."

"Of course." The fair-haired woman was already moving to support her sister.

Bree guided them to the cushion in the east. As Kat eased her sister onto the seat, a soft knock sounded. Fergus opened the door, a third purple cushion in hand. With a smile, Bree gathered the cushion from him and closed the door before turning back to face the sisters.

"Kat, here is one for you."

After seeing the two women seated in the east, Bree settled onto the cushion in the west. Looking at the two sisters she realized, Pamela's wispy energy was all but invisible in her sister's vibrant energy field. She wondered if Pamela would collapse without the strength of her sister's presence. *No wonder she insisted Kat be present for the journey.*

Under most circumstances, Bree discouraged clients from bringing friends or family members into journey sessions. The wisdom and guidance Spirit offered during a shamanic healing session was deeply personal. The information disclosed often exposed a quality or pattern still hidden to the client herself. To have someone bear witness to such stark and unflinching revelations often proved uncomfortable and intrusive. Bree had even seen friendships irrevocably transformed from the experience.

But Pamela had insisted. As Bree watched the orange light of Kat's energy field wrap around the dark-haired woman like a blanket, Bree understood. Kat was keeping her sister alive.

I wonder if Pamela knows.

Bree smiled at the two women. "I believe Fergus told you I am a healer?" The two women nodded. "That is true. While what we do appears very different on the surface, how we heal is essentially the same. We both help your body, mind and soul communicate so they can work together harmoniously again." Her eyes sought and found Pamela's. "Are you familiar with shamanism?"

Pamela shook her head.

"Shamanism is an earth-based spirituality. As old as humankind and as diverse, shamanic traditions view life as consisting of This World—the world of the physical, what we can see, smell, hear, taste and touch—and of the Otherworld—the world of the unseen, of the soul. Two halves of one whole, This World and the Otherworld need each other. They flow one into the other and determine what is possible in one and the other.

"To affect any kind of change, of healing, you need to shift something. Sometimes you can cause the desired change by altering something here in This World. Other times, no matter how many things you replace, reconfigure or vary on This Side, the pattern remains the same. In those situations, the shift must be made in the Otherworld, on the soul side of the relationship. That's where I can help."

Bree paused. Soft white light blinked and rippled around the edges of the room. In her inner vision, Bree watched the thin filaments stretch to enfold this circle of three. *Love, Love, Love*, her soul whispered into the forming circle.

She let her gaze drift from sister to sister, waiting for understanding to shine clear in their eyes. When that spark finally flared to life before her, she continued.

"I am what my tradition calls a *Bean feasa*, a wise woman, or what others would call a shamanic healer. My training in shamanic journey techniques allows me to shift my consciousness and walk in the Otherworld. I carry your question, your concern to the Wisdom Keepers on the Otherside so healing can flow. In essence, I function as an interpreter. I speak both your language and Their language, and through me the two of you communicate." She smiled. *Love, Love, Love.* "With your permission, of course."

Her eyes caught Pamela's. "Do I have your permission?"

The woman nodded. "Yes."

Bree held the shrinking woman's gaze. "You must understand—I can make no promises. We may ask what healing serves your soul's highest good. But, if the answer is none, I must abide by that response and do nothing."

Pamela shivered. Tears welled in the dark-haired woman's eyes.

"How could that possibly be the answer?" Kat's voice pushed into the silence. "My sister is clearly ill. Surely, something can be done."

Bree shifted her gaze to rest upon the fair-haired sister. "Death is not an illness, Kat. It is the ultimate conclusion of each physical lifetime, a journey each birth requires."

Kat's mouth gaped. "How can you say that?"

Bree settled more deeply into her cushion. "Unlike Western society, shamanic cultures embrace death as a part of life. They view death as a kind of graduation, a process of rebirth, the end of one mode of existence and the beginning of another. The soul releases its link to the physical body and returns to the Otherworld, to living as pure essence."

She shifted her gaze back to Pamela. "Death is not a failure. It is a doorway, a moment of completion which begins the next phase of life."

"You can't possibly..."

Pamela placed her hand upon her sister's arm. At her touch, the fair-haired woman fell silent.

"It's okay." Pamela's soft voice rasped. "I understand. But, if something may be done, I would like to try."

Bree caught and held the empty gaze until the woman shrugged.

"I am not afraid of death," Pamela whispered. "But I am not ready to die."

14

"Then let us begin."

With a nod, Bree slid her hand into the cloth drum bag just to her right. She pulled out a four-ounce, clear-glass canning jar half-full of water. Bree unscrewed the metal top and slid it back into her drum bag. Then she placed the open jar of water onto the low, wooden table, just to the left of the white candle in the crescent-shaped holder.

Bree dipped the three middle fingers of her right hand into the water. White light flooded her inner vision. For a moment, she was back in Ireland, kneeling before the sacred well of her Otherworldly Teacher, the goddess Bríghid.

"Take of these, my waters," Bríghid's voice whispered from the past to flow anew within Bree. *"Carry them with you always and know—like my Love, these waters are ever bathing you."*

Bree closed her eyes and touched her fingers to her heart, her lips, her forehead. As the waters of Bríghid's well washed over her, Bríghid's voice echoed through her. *"You are my Love. You are my Love. You are my Love."*

Resting her hands over her heart, Bree bowed to the waters. *Blessed is the Mother. Blessed is the Mystery. Sin é.*

Bree opened her eyes and slid her right hand back into her drum bag. She withdrew a ceramic tea bowl and set it on the floor in front of her. Reaching into the bag a third time, she took out a dime-sized piece of charcoal and a small chunk of amber-colored resin.

She looked up at the women. "Are either of you allergic to frankincense or incense of any kind?"

The two women shook their heads.

"Excellent."

Once again, Bree reached into her cloth drum bag, this time in search of the lighter she kept tucked in the small, interior pocket. Her fingertips found it easily and she slid it into her palm.

With her left hand, she placed the bowl on the right side of the table, leaving the candle in the middle. As she withdrew the lighter from the bag, she picked up the charcoal in her left hand. En route to the ceramic bowl, she lit the charcoal and placed it in the ceramic tea bowl. After blowing on the charcoal to bring it to full heat, she dropped the small chunk of frankincense resin on top of it. A thin wisp of sweet-scented smoke curled into the air before her.

Bree exhaled. As her breath fanned the burning charcoal, the resin bubbled. Dense smoke drifted skyward in silent blessing. Bree closed her eyes. *Love, Love, Love.*

Opening her eyes, Bree lit the candle. *Mother Brighid, bless this flame. Let this flame shine the light of your Love into this room, this circle, this Working this day. Shelter, support and imbue this Working with your healing Peace. Sin é.*

Brilliant, white light flashed, radiating outward from the center of the candle flame and spilling through the room to enfold Bree and the two sisters in a shimmering circle.

Bree closed her eyes. "Peace be in this space... Peace be in this circle..." Bree knew these words so well. They flowed effortlessly, like the light streaming to fill the room. "Peace be in this Working..."

She paused to breathe deeply. Around her the room softened into quiet, into the Grace of Peace. Allowing her awareness to expand to the directions, she called to the *Airds*, to the sacred directions of the Celtic Wheel of Life.

"Great Spirit of North, the home of earth and the wisdom of remembering... Great Spirit of the North I call to you in Peace. Come, join this circle. Shelter and hold this circle in the Grace of Your Love."

The air shifted. A subtle change flowed through the north of the room. Bree paused, waiting until an energetic wall arched firmly from her left to the two women sitting opposite her. Bree bowed her head in gratitude, then continued, drawing the protective circle *deiseal*, sunwise with the power of life-affirming creation.

"Great Spirit of East, the home of air and the wisdom of birthing... Great Spirit of East I call to you in Peace. Come, join this circle. Shelter and hold this circle in the Grace of Your Love."

Again, the air shifted. That subtle pressure spread through the east of the room, arching behind the two sisters. Offering silent gratitude, Bree bowed her head and allowed her awareness to flow sunwise to her right, past the women and into the south.

"Great Spirit of South, the home of fire and the wisdom of becoming... Great Spirit of South I call to you in Peace. Come, join this circle. Shelter and hold this circle in the Grace of Your Love."

That familiar, rippling pressure expanded and curved to almost touch Bree's right knee. Again Bree bowed her head in silent gratitude before allowing her awareness to flow ever sunward, into the west.

"Great Spirit of West, the home of water and the wisdom of returning... Great Spirit of West I call to you in Peace. Come, join this circle. Shelter and hold this circle in the Grace of Your Love."

That wall of pressure arched behind Bree. Holding her focus, she drew the shield back to north, to full circle.

"Great Spirit of Center, the home of ether and the wisdom of Sovereignty... Great Spirit of Center I call to you in Peace. Come, join this circle. Shelter and hold this circle in the Grace of Your Love."

Opalescent light blazed outward. Etching the circumference, the light sealed the circle and cleared the space for Working.

"Great Mother, Sacred Three, bless this Working. Guide this Working with the Love, the Wisdom, the Peace of your Grace."

In her inner vision, Bree watched the final words of the ritual ripple through the newly-formed circle. Sealing its edges, the blessing shimmered around her and the two sisters while brilliant, white light bathed them from the candle flame at the circle's center.

Eyes still closed, Bree reached to her left. Wrapping her fingers around the familiar wooden handle of her *bodhrán*, she drew the drum before her. As her right hand traced slow, droning circles across the hide, she peered through slitted eyes at the dark-haired woman seated in the east.

Pamela, she breathed the woman's name into the Otherworld. *What wisdom, guidance or healing serves Pamela's highest good and greatest healing this day?*

The low, moaning throb of the drum reverberated through Bree and her body swayed. Caught in the spiraling pull, she exhaled. As her eyes fell closed, she slipped into the Otherworld.

15

Bare feet sink into soft, thick moss. Leaning slightly forward, Bree opens her eyes. Red and orange leaves fall upon her half-hidden feet as something heavy pulls at her wrists and shoulders.

Her gaze tracks up her legs, up her woolen cloak, then pauses. The purple, cloth-covered bundle from her dream sits nestled in her arms. Runic glyphs flow the length of the leather thong binding the bundle. The ancient symbols rush like a river before her eyes. Struggling to read them, she squints and bends closer.

Twigs snap and leaves rustle behind Bree as men's voices echo in the distance. They call back and forth between groups, their voices encircling Bree like a net.

Her breath hangs thick upon the damp air and uncertainty shivers through her. Her eyes scanning the trees around her, she gathers the bundle tighter to her chest, pivots and stops short. The wild eyes of the woman from her dream hold her.

The woman steps toward her. "You must help me."

Three men call from the forest. Their voices rustle the trees behind Bree and, for a moment, her neck seems to burn with the heat of their breath.

The woman from her dream tenses. Terror floods the woman's eyes and grips Bree's throat.

Eyes fixed upon the woman, Bree calls mentally—Allies, be with me. Show me the wisdom, guidance or healing offered to Pamela this day for her highest good and greatest healing.

A breeze ripples the leaves of the trees, exhaling a blessing to encircle Bree and the woman. As the encompassing circle seals itself, a familiar voice cries through the Otherworld.

"Crrruck!"

Midnight-black wings stretch and press against unseen currents. Hugging the bundle to her chest, Bree lifts her gaze and meets that of her Raven Ally. Black, white and red light weaves through Bree. In a breath, she and her Ally are one.

Her arms stretch taut against the currents as her body leans, pressing in a spiral downward, downward, downward. The deep, musky scent of damp earth floods her senses and she rasps. Drawing her wings back, she opens her talons and grasps a felled branch of wood as she lands. She hops once, twice, to better her grip. Then, settling her feathers around her, she turns piercing, black eyes upon the woman before her.

"Crrruck!"

Bree shudders and inhales sharply. Her awareness again her own, she turns her gaze with Raven's, upon the woman from her dream.

Wild eyes dart from Bree to Raven and back again.

Raven's unblinking eyes narrow. Her feathers bristle and she shudders before throwing herself back into the air.

Midnight-black wings pump before Bree, pulling her Ally upward, until a familiar prickling stings Bree's left shoulder. As Raven alights, Bree pulls her head out of the way.

Glistening black eyes study the bundle in Bree's arms. Raven tilts her head and her eyes scan the runic inscriptions. Purple sparks sear along the edges of the glyphs and, one by one, they hiss and sizzle. Raven bristles and clacks her beak.

"What was stolen must be returned."

"Stolen?" Bree turns her head to the left and stares into the eye of her Raven Ally.

"Yes, Raven Child."

Bree drops her gaze to the bundle in her arms, then lifts her eyes to meet those of the woman. "This parcel does not belong to you?"

The woman's eyes jump from Bree to the bundle to Raven. As the woman's body tenses, Bree wonders if she will run. Instead, she glares at Bree and juts her chin.

"The parcel is mine."

"But what it contains is not." Raven narrows her eyes.

Bree and Raven stare at the woman. Eyes glaring, the woman's hands ball into fists, then release slowly.

"No." Her voice bites, low and menacing.

Raven shudders on Bree's shoulder, then draws her feathers down around her. Bree turns her gaze toward her Ally and Raven's black eye meets hers.

"What was stolen must be returned."

"How?" Bree glances down at the bundle, then back at her Ally. "In Peace, in Love and for the highest good, how?"

Raven taps the purple cloth with the tip of her beak. "Come, follow me."

The woman clenches her hands into fists and steps in front of Bree. As the woman's eyes close, she slowly extends her hand and a wall of heat blazes toward Bree.

Raven whispers in Bree's ear. "Steady, Raven Child."

Bree sends energetic roots shooting deep into the earth of the Otherworld. Bear, she calls mentally, send me your strength.

Invisible paws press tenderly upon Bree's chest. As an unseen, leather snout snuffles against her nose, the voice of her Bear Ally echoes through Bree. "Inhale my breath and stand untouched."

Bree draws in a slow, deep breath, her eyes focused on the hand now reaching toward her. "I thought you wanted my help."

The woman's hand inches steadily closer, until it hovers above the leather strap. The wall of heat intensifies and small flames spark and curl around Bree's energetic field. The woman opens her eyes and glares into Bree's.

Bree raises her eyebrows but says nothing. She inhales another slow, deep breath from her Bear Ally.

The flames grow hotter, licking and lashing Bree's energy field with long, jagged tongues. As the blaze curls well clear of her, Bree stands and draws in another deep breath from Bear.

Leaves crackle as Bree's Stag Ally bounds through the forest to land directly behind the woman. He thumps his front hoof upon the soft earth, then drops his head and shakes his antlers. His eyes lock on the woman's back and he grunts.

"Rrrugh!"

The woman whirls toward the unexpected sound. Releasing her control of the wall of heat, it rebounds off Bree's energy field and slams into the woman. Her body lunges forward and her feet slip on the soft undergrowth. As she falls to the ground, the flames rush over her back and she cries out loud.

Small clouds of smoke drift past Bree, obscuring her view. As they clear, she sees her Stag Ally. Muscles bristling, his front hooves root into the soft moss. He holds his head lowered and perfectly still, his antlers aimed menacingly at the woman on the ground.

Bree bows her head to Stag, offering silent gratitude for her Ally's protection. Then she glances at Raven on her left shoulder. With a nod of approval from Raven, Bree takes a step toward the unmoving form.

She watches the woman's chest rise and fall. Reassured the woman is still alive, Bree scans upward along the woman's body and frowns. The skin on the woman's neck is seared bright red.

"You are injured."

"It's nothing." The woman pushes herself up to her knees and sits, her back to Bree. Dark patches of singed linen dot the woman's woven dress.

Bree narrows her eyes. "You are in serious trouble."

The woman jerks at Bree's soft voice and raises terrified eyes to Bree.

"Others are dying because of you. Because of what you have done. Including my client." Bree bends her knees and crouches to look at the woman eye to eye. "You know it. And when I take this back," she gestures to the cloth-covered bundle in her hands, "everyone else will know it, too."

The woman's hands clench into fists as the sound of a young girl crying spills through Bree.

"That's why you attacked me, even after you asked for my help." Bree raises her eyebrows. "I am correct, aren't I?"

The woman scowls, then turns her back to Bree once more. Stag leans closer, his antlers poised and threatening, but the woman only shrugs. "It doesn't matter anymore."

Bree rises to standing. "If that is so, are you ready to do what needs to be done for healing to flow?"

The woman hunches over her knees and rocks herself, arms clutched around her belly. When she says nothing, Bree sighs.

"Very well. If you insist on refusing the healing offered, I will leave you to your alternative." Bowing slightly, Bree touches her right hand to her forehead in honoring. As she rises, Raven lifts herself into flight.

"Crrruck! But what was stolen must be returned. This way, Raven Child."

Bare feet rustling leaves, Bree follows her Ally deeper into the forest. The weight of the bundle pulls at her and she shifts her hold to ease the growing ache in her left shoulder. Once again, her eyes drift over the runes etched across the leather thong and she wonders what the arcane glyphs could mean.

All around her, ancient trees stretch half-bare branches into the fading light. No path marks her way. Glancing up, she adjusts her steps to follow Raven.

"Wait!"

Bree stops. Footsteps crunch upon the forest floor until the woman's breath hangs in a heavy mist to Bree's right. Without a word, Bree casts her gaze upon the woman.

The woman shakes her head. "I am not ready to die."

16

Orange, red and gold leaves rustle beneath Bree's bare feet. Once more, she glances over her left shoulder. The woman is still there, plodding several paces behind Bree, as if she were being dragged unwillingly.

"Crrruck!"

Bree lifts her gaze to the sky. Her Raven Ally circles overhead, then banks to the right on outstretched wings. Returning her gaze to the forest, Bree adjusts her path through the woods to follow Raven. She begins to turn her head to look behind her, then pauses. The crackling leaves confirm —the woman is still there.

Tracking deeper into the forest, darkness thickens around Bree and she shivers in the chill, damp air. Her gaze drifts along the deep ridges of the ancient bark and up endless branches. The trees grow closer together here, so close their branches seem to wrap around the neighboring trunks. For a moment, her vision blurs and she sees the forest as a great tapestry, a woven fabric of living, pulsing, life.

She blinks and the golden leaves of the autumn forest wink back at her. Her breath billowing clouds upon the air, she pauses and looks around her.

The forest is quiet now. She can hear the rasp of her breath, the soft thuft of Raven's wings above her and the muffled thump of the woman's reluctant steps behind her.

"Crrruck! Crrruck! Crrruck!"

"Coming," Bree exhales.

She turns to follow Raven along a narrow path through dense overgrowth. She places her feet carefully, threading her way between a cluster of ancient rowan trees. With each step, silence grows until it swallows every sound. Bree longs to ask Raven what this place is, but the silence hushes her.

She bends down to step under a low-hanging branch. As she rises to standing, opalescent moonlight spills upon her face. Grateful, she closes her eyes and drinks in the light.

Smiling softly, Bree opens her eyes. Around her stretches an enormous nemeton—a perfectly round clearing in the woods. She scans the quarter of its vast circumference arching before her. Wherever she looks, the trees grow almost on top of each other, creating an all but solid periphery. Letting her gaze drift along the ancient limbs, she wonders just how old this forest must be.

"Too old to remember..." the trees breathe their reply.

Bree bows her head. "Blessed is the Mystery."

"This way, Raven Child."

Bree turns toward her Raven Ally's voice and inhales sharply. At the center of the clearing, a village drinks in the blanketing light.

"What is this place?" Bree's voice is a whisper.

"This was once a thriving community." Raven circles above Bree's head. "Now, only one remains."

A hand falls hard upon Bree's right shoulder and the woman pushes past Bree with a grunt. "I know the way."

"Go." Midnight-black wings stretch and spiral above Bree. "Follow her."

Bree nods and, shifting the bundle in her arms, steps into the nemeton. The grass is warm under her feet. Smiling, she slows her pace. After the damp chill of the forest, the gentle warmth seems luxurious.

A few strides carry her to the edge of the village. A well-worn, earthen path opens to her left and curves sunwise, disappearing between small, wooden structures. Following the woman, Bree steps onto the earthen path.

A deep, droning tone reverberates beneath her. Rising from the earth, it surges up her legs. As she bends with the first curve, the tone flows into her pelvis.

The path arcs sunwise again, spiraling toward the center of the village. Small, round, wooden homes stretch to either side of the narrow track. As the tone pools within her belly, Bree lets her gaze drift across the structures. No smoke rises from the thatched roofs and she realizes, they are empty.

A narrow lane branches off the main pathway and Bree slows as she passes. She leans to see where the lane leads. To her surprise, a few feet away it flows sunwise, forming a snug cul de sac. Small, single-story, earthen roundhouses hug the edges of the pooling lane. But, once again, no smoke rises from their roofs. No songs of life spill from their doorways. The deep toning, now coursing along Bree's arms, is the only sound of life.

Bree returns her focus to the path ahead of her. In the distance, the woman disappears around another curve. Bree hastens to follow her. A few quick strides and she catches sight of the woman's back just before it vanishes around a sudden bend. Tightening her hold on the bundle under her left arm, Bree quickens her pace.

Her feet track the spiraling pathway and she steps into an open cul de sac. The earthen structures of the heart of the village spill around her in a perfect circle. Beneath her feet, the earth vibrates with the humming tone.

Bare feet kissing the earth of the cul de sac, the deep toning rushes upward. It floods her head then showers out her crown, pouring over her in spirals of black, red and white light. As the waves cascade through her energy field, Bree closes her eyes and trembles in awe.

"Blessed is the Mother. Blessed is the Mystery," she whispers.

"Crrruck! Crrruck! Crrruck!"

Raven's cry pulses with the toning and Bree opens her eyes. A solitary woman stands in the center of the cul de sac. A purple cloak enfolds the woman from head to foot. As her auburn hair shimmers in the moonlight, a hand emerges from beneath the cloth and presses upon the woman's heart as she bows.

"Síocháin duit," the woman's voice ripples across the open space as she rises to standing. "Peace be upon you."

The parcel balanced in the crook of her left arm, Bree returns the bow.

"*Peace be between us.*" As she rises to standing, Bree's eyes meet those of the woman.

They finish the ancient greeting together. "*Now and through all time.*"

The deep toning wanes, sinking back into the earth and exhaling silence through the cul de sac.

As the woman walks slowly toward her, Bree lets her gaze drift down the length of the woman's cloak. Runic glyphs cascade in spiraling waves of black, red and white along the left edge of the purple cloth. When the woman is close enough to notice the gesture, Bree shifts her gaze and stares at the bundle in her arms.

They are the same, Bree notes mentally, both the cloth and the style of the etchings.

The voice of her Raven Ally whispers through her. "*Yes, Raven Child.*"

The woman stops several paces in front of Bree. Heat rushes down Bree's chest and she turns to face the woman. Green eyes trace the edge of Bree's woolen cloak, then rise to meet Bree's with a smile.

"*Gentle blessings upon thee, Daughter of the Chalice.*" The woman pauses as her eyes scan the bundle in Bree's arms. "*What seek you in this place?*"

Bree leans her head to the side, allowing Raven to settle onto her left shoulder. With a nod from her Ally, Bree faces the woman. "*Priestess of the Goddess, I seek healing for the highest good of one known to me. I come on her behalf, at her request. To that end, I seek to return that which was stolen.*"

Bree shifts the parcel into both hands and holds it out before her. "*Tell me, Priestess, do you recognize this bundle?*"

The woman stiffens. Cold fire blazes in her green eyes. "*Deirdre.*" She heaves a sigh. "*Come out child. I know this is your doing.*"

17

Shadows swirl in the moonlight spilling before Bree. The shifting movement chafes like sandpaper down her left arm and she turns, seeking the source of the irritation.

Her gaze snaps to the obscured edges of two roundhouses. In the drifting darkness, she can just distinguish the lurking outline of the woman Bree encountered in the forest. Following Bree's gaze, the priestess turns her head toward the shadows.

Deirdre steps into the moonlight. Her eyes narrowing in defiance, she lifts her chin and glares at the priestess. Deirdre's voice pummels the cul de sac. "At least I did something."

"But at what cost, my child? At what cost?" The cloaked woman sighs and shakes her head. Her auburn hair sparkles in the Otherworldly moonlight, casting spirals of black, red and white light across the cul de sac.

She presses her lips into a thin line and offers Dierdre a brusque glance. Then, looking away, she takes a step toward Bree.

"I am the Priestess of this Spiral. My name is now one with the Goddess, the Great Mother of Life. You may address me simply as Sister." She bows her head and raises her hands to her sides, palms facing Bree. "Speak your question and hear the wisdom of the Goddess."

Raven rubs her beak across Bree's left cheek. "Ask, Raven Child, and let healing flow."

Bree again extends the bundle before her. "Sister, how may what was stolen be peacefully returned that healing may flow for the highest good of my client and for the highest good of all involved?"

The priestess steps forward and places her left hand upon the bundle. Opalescent light shimmers across the purple covering and down the leather thong. The runic glyphs sizzle and hiss as short flames erupt along their edges. The priestess jerks her hand from the bundle, steam rising from her palm. With a shudder, she looks at Bree.

"The item contained within the parcel you carry belongs rightfully to the spiral of men beyond this wood."

"They hunt us like dogs." Deirdre's voice cuts between Bree and the priestess.

Green eyes flashing, the priestess gestures toward the bundle. "Now, it would seem, with good reason."

Deirdre scowls and folds her arms across her chest.

The priestess straightens her shoulders. "Be ye not deceived, child. You have done no one any kindness here." She gestures toward Bree. "Least of all this innocent soul."

From under furrowed brows, Deirdre glowers.

"You have made a liar out of me." The priestess' voice is ice. "I gave them my word—my Oath—that this," she points to the bundle, "was not in our possession."

Deirdre shrugs. "And so it wasn't. They assaulted us anyway. This," she hisses, pointing to the bundle in Bree's hands, "at least affords us power and protection."

"You are wrong, child." The priestess shakes her head, sorrow glinting in her green eyes. "A Hallow wrongly taken always yields Unraveling. Only Right Relationship may birth Balance and Healing. Anything else leads to illness and death. As, it seems, your soul is learning."

"Fine!" Deirdre throws her arms up in the air. "I will take it back to them."

Raven clacks her beak as the priestess shakes her head. "No, child." The priestess' voice flows tenderly. "They would kill you on sight. By stealing

68

this, it has marked you. They will see its imprint upon your soul immediately. No, you will find no shelter in their hall."

Warmth spreads across Bree's left cheek as her Raven Ally nuzzles it with her head. "Go." Raven's voice is soft in Bree's ear. "Go restore Balance and let healing flow."

Bree tilts her head closer to Raven and whispers mentally. *You are certain?*

"Go, Bree Nic Bhríde, Mo Ghrá... my Love." Bríghid's voice ripples through Bree. "Go with my blessing."

Bree sighs and tucks the bundle back under her left arm. "I will go."

"Yes," slowly the priestess nods. "You are an outsider here, beyond the bounds of this dispute. That, and your status as Healer, will protect you. But," she pauses to smile. "As Priestess of this Spiral, this is my responsibility. I shall go with you."

"No!" Deirdre steps between Bree and the priestess. "You must not. You are needed here." She gestures to the village around them. "Alive."

"Needed here?" The priestess pivots sunwise, her eyes scanning the empty roundhouses. When she faces Deirdre again, she shrugs. "By whom?"

"But, if you are lost..." Deirdre takes a step closer to the priestess. "We have no second to replace you."

The priestess presses her palm tenderly to Deirdre's cheek. "If I am lost, you will not need to replace me." With a half smile, she releases her hand back to her side. "It is my duty to go, to free the others and you."

Deirdre opens her mouth to protest, but the priestess hushes her with a look. Heaving a sigh, Deirdre closes her eyes. She slumps forward and her chin droops toward the ground.

The priestess rests her hands on Deirdre's shoulders. "Trust in the Goddess." She kisses Deirdre's forehead, then looks at Bree. "Come, follow me."

18

"Is there no other way?"

The bundle tucked securely in her arms, Bree crouches half-hidden in a cluster of alder trees near the edge of the men's clearing in the forest. Her Raven Ally perches on the branch just to her left. Raven's black eyes shimmer in the shadows, locked, with Bree's, on the village.

"None." To Bree's right, the priestess peeks at the clustered buildings from behind the trunk of an aspen tree. "That road is the only point of entry. As the main road, it leads directly to the central circle and the hall of the High King. From there, smaller lanes spiral outward to the peripheries."

Bree frowns. "Seems an odd plan for a village, even a small one."

The priestess withdraws to stand fully concealed behind the ancient tree. "It is the way of the Masculine, to spiral outward. Just as it is the way of the Feminine to spiral inward." Bree faces the priestess, who nods. "We live according to our natures."

Light shimmers in Bree's inner vision. As the forest around her falls away, opalescent moonlight spills to fill her view. Spiraling and swirling, it dances before Bree. Then a single ray of golden sunlight flashes, piercing the dance with its radiance. The two colors twirl, spinning around each other as they spiral sunwise. Their dance quickens. A heartbeat pulses, and moonlight and sunlight throb together as one.

The rhythm steadies the dance. Moonlight and sunlight swirl, two halves of one whole, aching, yearning, reaching for each other in that endless, turning pulsation.

Bree blinks. Darkness spills, filling moonlight's half of the swirling circle. Before her eyes, a black teardrop reaches as the sunlight half pulses from golden to white. The whiteness stretches, arching into another teardrop nestled alongside the black teardrop. Together, the two pulse and turn as a perfect circle.

"The Tao," Bree exhales.

Bríghid's voice ripples through her. "The Feminine and the Masculine in harmonious co-creation."

The rushing song of the heartbeat floods through Bree. In that pulsing, the black teardrop swells. With each beat, it grows until it presses against the boundary of the circle.

But the heartbeat throbs on, driven by and driving the dance of co-creation.

The blackness shivers, its energies swirling inward upon itself and pressing into a single point of stillness. Light erupts from that point, cascading outward as the black teardrop yields to the white, as stillness becomes action and potential births manifestation.

Brilliant white light pours into the circle, pulsing and throbbing as the heartbeat presses onward. Like the blackness before it, the white floods the circle until it strains against the boundary containing it.

Still the heartbeat throbs on, singing its sacred song of co-creation.

Shivering, the whiteness rushes inward upon itself, driving itself into a single, pooling point. As action reaches its apex, it yields to stillness and blackness spills from that point to seep into the circle again.

And all the while, the heartbeat pulses.

It shudders through Bree. Before her, the spilling blackness stretches, extending thin tendrils into the circle. Curving and curling, they thicken to form a black dragon. Bree blinks. Where the black and white teardrops turned their eternal circle, now two dragons—one black, the other white— chase each other's tails.

Bree smiles. "Like the dragons on the door of Fergus' clinic."

"Exactly," *Raven's voice whispers through her.*

A green eye opens and the black dragon winks. "Welcome back, Bree Nic Bhríde."

The green eye rolls forward and stares at the tail before it. As the white dragon opens a shining red eye, the black and the white dragons reach with open mouths and swallow each other. Opalescent light flashes, revealing a solitary black spot.

"The dot," the goddess Bríghid whispers. "She is the beginning, the Great Source, the Divine Feminine and Her womb of potential."

Golden light flashes within the dot, then stretches outward. Shimmering, it reaches as a single line of golden light.

"The line is the Divine masculine," Bríghid's voice ripples through Bree. "He is activation drawing potential from Source outward into Manifestation."

The golden light flashes, blazing outward and filling Bree's awareness. Bree blinks her eyes against the brilliance as Bríghid's voice whispers. "And as such, the Divine Masculine prefers the direct approach."

Her vision clearing, the forest reappears around Bree. She glances up at her Raven Ally. Black eyes glistening, Raven nods.

Bree shifts her gaze to the solitary road leading into the men's village. For a moment, golden light shimmers, etching a perfect line and illuminating the path.

She sighs. "Very well. A straight line it is, then. The Divine Feminine honoring the Divine Masculine."

19

Pinpoint prickles sting Bree's energy field as the growing crowd of men scan her with questioning eyes. One by one the men appear out the doorways and side alleys that stretch along the central, earthen path.

Placing her bare feet carefully, Bree watches another man duck under a thatch overhang as he exits the small, wooden dwelling to her right. Curious, grey eyes peer from a weather-chiseled face and fix upon her. Wiping his hands with a dark cloth, he steps onto the pathway and joins the men now trailing behind Bree.

Heat sears the soles of her feet. For a moment, Bree wonders if the dry earth of the path has become red-hot coals or sun-baked sands. She considers dropping her gaze, if only to see for herself the source of the flames rising up her legs, scorching her knees and engulfing her pelvis.

But a black-haired man in warrior leathers leers at her. His mocking smirk alarms her and she cannot look away, even as he falls into step with the men behind her. Watching the man—and the ever-growing crowd—from the corner of her eyes, Bree nestles the bundle more securely under her left arm.

Raven's voice rasps low in Bree's ear.

Bree's eyes dart to her Ally, perched on her left shoulder. Raven sits *utterly still, black eyes gleaming in the cascading sunlight. Bree inhales slowly, then casts a glance to the priestess walking slightly behind and to Bree's right. Shoulders rigid, the woman's green eyes scan the men filling the road around them. Bree clenches her teeth. The tension in the woman's shoulders reinforces Bree's own inner foreboding.*

Men's voices rumble around her. Echoing from all sides, they pummel her like hungry growls from pacing animals. Bree places another bare foot upon the earth. Peace, she whispers through her soul, I come in Peace.

Someone behind her coughs. Startled, Bree peers over her right shoulder and inhales deeply.

As far as she can see, men fill the roadway behind her. The path back to the forest is blocked completely. Holding her breath, Bree shudders. The only way open now is forward.

She stiffens and glances into Raven's steely black gaze. "I sure hope you are right about this."

"Remember who you are." Raven's voice echoes through her.

Fire rushes up Bree's torso. As the blaze scalds her neck, it pours down her shoulders and out her hands. In her inner vision, small, red-orange flames burst from her palms. Breathing into the blue flame of her soul, she shifts the bundle in her arms.

Another row of thatched houses falls away and Bree steps into an open square. To both her left and right, narrow lanes reach from each of the four corners into the distance only to disappear behind more thatched houses.

But Bree's eyes are drawn to the center of the square. There, atop a dais and under an intricately-woven, sloping roof, a single man sits upon a gilded chair.

Bare feet burning, Bree takes another step toward the dais and the man raises golden eyes to hers.

A scorching flame bursts from the ground and races up the length of her. Letting her head fall backward, Bree closes her eyes. She draws the flame into her, then exhales sharply. Long, red-orange flames trail out of her mouth and dissipate into the air above her.

Cool air drifts across her skin, spilling Goddess bumps along her flesh, and Bree smiles. "Blessed is the Mystery," she whispers.

Raven nudges her ear. "He is the High King of this Spiral. Wait for him to acknowledge you before speaking."

Opening her eyes, Bree lifts her head and meets, again, the golden gaze of the king. To her right, the priestess shudders.

With a glance in her direction, Bree understands her distress. The men of the village swarm around them. A dense wall of bodies, they seal off the square and block all possible retreat.

Their voices rumble around Bree as the men step closer, locking Bree and the priestess in the center of the square. Growled speculation pounds against Bree and the sound of clashing metal rings through her.

Bree returns her gaze to the king. Golden sunlight flashes and the man rises, silencing the crowd. He takes two steps and pauses.

Heat snaps the length of Bree's woolen cloak as the man scans the glyphs woven there. Then his eyes lock on the parcel under her left arm.

He steps off the dais and crosses the open area, heading directly for Bree. Eyes still locked on the bundle, he reaches his hand to hover, palm down, over the purple cloth. As he stops in front of Bree, golden light flashes from his hand.

It pours the length of the bundle, illuminating the runic glyphs one by one. To Bree's inner vision, the arcane symbols shiver and pull against the leather strap that binds them. Fire hisses and sparks sizzle, but the bundle remains intact.

Eyes narrowing, the man lowers his arm and lifts golden eyes to meet Bree's.

"Well met, Healer, that you should grace my Hall with such a gift. But, tell me—do you enter this place in Peace? Or should I expect some fight of ye?"

Bree bows her head and extends her right arm to her side, allowing her cloak to part far enough to reveal she carries no weapon.

"I come in Peace with the hope that Peace may flow between us, now and through all time. But," she lifts her head, "I must correct you."

The king's eyebrows rise.

Bree shakes her head. "I carry no gift."

The man presses his hands upon his hips and nods toward the bundle under Bree's left arm. "Then, what is that?"

Bree shifts her gaze to the bundle, before looking again at the king. "As a Healer, I seek only Jera—the restoration of Right Relationship in the Highest Good. To that end, I come to return what was stolen." Gripping the bundle with both hands, she holds it out toward him. Her hazel eyes lock on his. "I understand this belongs rightfully to you."

20

The High King reaches for the parcel. As his eyes alight on the priestess beyond Bree's right shoulder, he freezes. Eyes narrowing, he withdraws his hands and presses them upon his hips.

"Now then." He cocks his head and glares at Bree. "Just why should I trust you?"

Bree holds the parcel steady before her, extended toward the High King. "The markings on my cloak answer that question for me." She smiles into his cold face, her soul whispering Love, Love, Love. "I know you can read them."

The man scowls at the priestess, then folds his arms over his chest. "Insufficient."

Bree glances into Raven's black gaze and pleads silently—A little help, perhaps?

Thump, thump, thump! A deep, thudding sound reverberates through the crowded plaza as a thready voice calls, "Make way! Make way!"

Murmurs ripple through the crowd and feet rustle against the earthen surface of the road. Bree glances over her shoulder just as the throng parts and disgorges an old man. Stooped and leaning heavily on a gnarled, wooden branch, he pushes his way to Bree's right side. As Raven shivers on

79

Bree's shoulder, the old man wheezes noisily beside her. Through stringy, grey hair, he winks at Bree, then faces the High King.

Thump, thump, thump! The old man raps his walking stick on the earth and shouts into the crowd. "I vouch for this woman."

Shaking his head, the High King laughs. "Beauty has ye blinded, ye daft old man."

Fiery eyes narrow and the old man leans forward, preternaturally still, upon his walking stick. His voice rumbles deep and strong, belying his age. "Be careful who ye call daft, boy."

Lightning flashes and Bree blinks against the glare. Where the old man stood, shoulders broad enough to span the Missouri River now cover a torso the size of a house. Tracking the neck upward, Bree stares. Eyes glowering dangerously, the Dagda, the Great Father of the Celtic mystical tradition, stands beside her. The Long Mór, his club of death and healing, twitches in his hands.

With a small, strangled gasp, the High King bows. His voice is a whisper. "Forgive me, Great Father."

The Dagda drums his club against his palm, then grunts. "Very well."

The High King places his right hand over his heart and rises. With a nod to the Great Father, he faces Bree. "Be ye welcome in this Hall with my blessing of Peace."

"Thank you." Bree bows.

As she rises, the Dagda, disguised again as the grey-haired man leaning on his walking stick, pats her shoulder. "See, the Old Man comes through for you. Perhaps you will think better of me in the future."

Bree furrows her brow and opens her mouth to ask the Dagda what he means. But the High King lifts the parcel from her arms. At his touch, the contents hum.

He smiles, then looks up at Bree. "Truly, ye know not what this contains?"

Bree shakes her head. "I know only that it belongs here, in your care. Nothing more."

Frowning slightly, the High King glances at the Dagda, who nods solemnly.

Balancing the bundle in his left hand, the High King struggles to undo the leather thong. With each touch of his fingers, golden light runs the length of the runic glyphs. To Bree's inner vision, the symbols spit and hiss as they pull the strap more tightly closed.

The priestess steps forward, palms open and extended before her. "Please, allow me."

The High King backs away from the priestess. Grasping the bundle in both hands, he shifts it to his right, beyond her reach. From beside Bree, a threatening growl rumbles in the Dagda's throat.

With an exhale, the High King returns the cloth parcel before him.

The priestess gently lowers her fingertips to the binding and closes her eyes. Moonlight spills down the leather thong. As the glyphs dissolve in the shimmering light, the strap falls away and vanishes in a silvery flash.

Opening her eyes, the priestess grasps both ends of the purple cloth in her hands. She spreads it upon the ground and a short, ceremonial blade of gold sparkles in the sunlight.

Hushed voices murmur through the throng of men surrounding Bree. "The Blade of the Father..."

A man emerges from the crowd, a brilliant blue robe flowing from his shoulders to ankles. "My Lord." He bows to the High King, then gestures toward the golden blade. "With your permission."

"Of course."

Positioning his body well clear of the purple cloth, the man kneels beside the blade. He opens his palms and, whispering a prayer, runs them over the blade. From hilt to tip, wherever his hands hover, the blade gleams golden and an ethereal tone sings from the metal.

With a sigh, the man withdraws his hands. "It is untarnished, the proper Hallow of the Father still."

The High King gathers the blade into his hands. As he lifts it over his head, the blade sings into the plaza. All around Bree, the men tone back to it.

Bree shivers. "Blessed is the Mystery."

21

Men's voices wash over Bree. As the toning fills the square, golden light pulses along the blade. It throbs from hilt to point, then streams outward. Pooling in an ever-widening circle, it reaches to enfold the men still toning their song of honor.

Bree stands frozen, eyes fixed on the golden glow pouring toward her from the blade. "Mother Bríghid," she whispers through her pounding heart, "protect me."

The Dagda places his hand upon her right shoulder. "Come."

Bree turns and follows the Great Father of the Celtic tradition. Stooped and leaning heavily upon a gnarled, wooden staff, he parts the crowd with a wave of his hand. Bree taps the priestess' wrist and nods for her to follow. Despite his aged appearance, the Dagda sets a brisk pace and Bree lengthens her stride to match him.

Wave upon wave of men parts for them to pass, and Bree follows the Dagda deeper into that living sea. Swallowed in their tide, she is grateful for their closed eyes and faces upraised in song. She holds her breath until the last row of men opens and sunlight streams before her again. As the sea of men falls behind her, the gleaming green of the nemeton fills her view. Her eyes track the open pathway leading back to the ancient wood and Bree exhales.

"Wait."

Bree stiffens at the sound of the High King's voice. Placing her feet to maintain optimum balance, she pivots to face him and braces herself for a fight.

Tears glisten in the High King's eyes as he bows deeply. "Thank you."

Bree stifles a gasp, then bows in return. "Síocháin doibh... Peace be upon you. Peace be between us..."

The High King smiles and they finish the ritual together. "...Now and through all time."

Bree stands facing the High King, the sea of men spilling out behind him. Rolling through them, Bree can still hear their song of toning.

"Crrruck! Time to go, Raven Child."

Bree turns her head toward her Raven Ally, still perched upon her left shoulder. Then, with a nod to the priestess beside her, she follows the Dagda down the path and out of the village of men. As the trees of the ancient forest enfold her once more, Bree stops. Resting in the shelter of an enormous rowan tree, she leans against its trunk and exhales.

The priestess steps in front of Bree. "I must thank you."

Bree looks at the priestess and shrugs. "It is what we do. Surely, you know that."

"No." The priestess shakes her head. "You put yourself in danger to accomplish something that I and mine could not." She faces Bree. "I know it and will remember it."

The priestess' green eyes meet and hold Bree's. Silently, Bree nods.

"In the meantime," the priestess smiles, "may healing flow be restored."

Talons grip Bree's left shoulder. From her perch there, Raven ruffles her feathers and snaps her beak.

Bree frowns at her Ally's sudden outburst. She turns her head to ask Raven what more might need to be done to ensure Pamela's healing, but a deep, guttural chuckling interrupts her.

"Heh, heh, heh!"

"Grrrack!" With a start, Raven spreads midnight-black wings and launches herself from Bree's shoulder.

Massive fingers grasp Bree and the priestess behind their shoulders.

Pressed together, their feet dangle in the air as they rise. Bree turns her head to see the Dagda's laughing face.

Stringy, grey hair thickens before her eyes into dense, cascading waves. Bree blinks and a deep black coloring rises out of the roots. Flooding to the ends of the still-lengthening tips, it chases away the grey and spills past ever-widening shoulders.

Her dangling feet soar past the tops of the ancient trees. Stifling a gasp, Bree lifts her gaze back to the Dagda's face. Wrinkles soften into smooth, lustrous, flowing skin as the old man guise melts away and the Dagda's body swells to his giant appearance.

Releasing his grip, the Dagda drops Bree and the priestess. She falls, side by side with the priestess, past the club of death and healing, tucked securely into his belt, and lands in the open palm of his free hand.

"Heh, heh, heh!"

Bree and the priestess rise past the Dagda's shaking belly. Unable to balance on two feet, Bree drops to her knees and grips the trench-like creases of his palm. As darkness engulfs the edges of her vision, two, moon-sized, shining eyes loom into view. Bree shakes her head.

"Where are you taking us?'

"Home. Where else?" The Dagda chuckles. "You first, Priestess."

Beside Bree, the priestess rises into the air. Feet dangling against the encroaching darkness, two giant-sized fingers grasp the priestess' cloak behind her shoulders. Bree crawls to the edge of the Dagda's palm and peers through the deepening shadows toward the ground below her. To her surprise, the Dagda places the priestess gently into the center of her Spiral. Then, the terrain below Bree blurs.

"Now, you."

Bree clings to the folds in the Dagda's flesh as he lowers his hand to the ground. Jumping off his palm, Bree considers the ten, pale mounds just visible before her.

The mounds rise and fall in rapid succession as the Dagda wriggles his toes. "So," he kneels down to meet Bree's gaze, his grin flashing through her fading vision. "Friends?"

Bree gapes as darkness swallows her and pulls her slowly out of the

Otherworld. Her mouth still hanging open, she blinks and clears her throat.
"I never really thought I mattered to you."

The Dagda's voice rumbles from the dark. "Well, know this—you do."

22

"You are saying," Pamela spoke slowly, as if searching for each word, "I am related to this woman Deirdre?"

"That is correct." Bree considered the dark-haired woman before her in the flickering candlelight. For a moment, something about the shape of Pamela's eyes reminded her of Deirdre's. "She is a member of your Soul Family."

Kat shook her head. "I don't understand."

Bree smiled. "Just as we live in families on This Side of the Veil, souls gather into families in the Otherworld. What draws Soul Families together, however, is a little different.

"While human families are linked by genetics, by the shared DNA that is passed from generation to generation, Soul Families are united by a purpose. You see, each member of a Soul Family strives to awaken, cultivate, care-take or nurture a common vibration in the Universe. How each soul contributes to or interacts with that vibration may differ, but, in the end, the ultimate good of that vibration is at the heart of the existence of each member of the Soul Family."

Bree paused. Candlelight played across Pamela's face but Bree's client said nothing. With a nod, Bree continued.

"For example, souls dedicated to the Divine Feminine shape their communities in spirals. That way, from their foundations up, they live in right relationship with their soul's purpose. The very structure of their world—their homes, their streets, their community itself—flows with the spiraling energy of the Goddess. Souls like Deirdre." Bree looked into Pamela's eyes. "Like you."

Pamela's eyes gleamed in the room's flickering light. "Like me," she whispered.

"And because the actions of one member of a Soul Family directly impact all members of that community..."

Pamela spoke over Bree, "... Deirdre's choice to steal the men's blade affected me, made me ill."

"Correct." Bree nodded. "Stealing the Blade, the Hallow of the Divine Masculine, of the Father, disrupted the co-creative flow between the Divine Feminine and the Divine Masculine for Deirdre and her people. In fact, Deirdre's choice reversed the flow. Where life force once flowed outward into the world, after the theft, life force was consumed, drained away from the world. As a result, the vitality of all members of Deirdre's Soul Family waned, including yours, Pamela."

"But Deirdre wasn't ill." Kat's voice bellowed, shattering the quiet of the circle. "She stole the object. Why did her life force remain intact?"

Bree flinched. Her face stung, as if Pamela's sister had reached out and slapped her. *Love, Love, Love,* her soul whispered. "I don't know."

Kat glared across the altar at her.

"You ask an excellent question, one I would love to be able to answer." Bree shook her head. "But, I cannot. Perhaps her contact with the Hallow protected her. Perhaps her position within the Soul Spiral redirected the effect to the others. I don't know. The journey did not clarify this and I cannot explain it either."

Kat took a breath. Bree braced herself for another onslaught, but Pamela's soft voice spoke first.

"What is a Hallow?"

Bree shifted her gaze to the dark-haired woman across from her.

"A Hallow is a physical item imbued with divine energy so it becomes the living embodiment of that energy. Its own vibration is overwritten with the vibration of another—the Goddess, the God, Truth, for example. And once infused with the new vibration, the item *becomes* that which has imbued it. From that moment on, to come into contact with that item, that Hallow, is to be in the presence of Its imbuing divinity.

"The Blade is a Hallow of the Divine Masculine. To stand in Its presence is the same as standing before the Great Father. To touch It is to come into direct contact with the God."

Kat frowned. "But, you said Deirdre lived in a Soul Spiral dedicated to the Divine Feminine, to the Goddess."

"That is correct." Bree gazed at the crescent-shaped candleholder on the altar. "Which only intensified the consequences of the theft. Deirdre had no right to appeal to the Blade, much less to take It for her own purposes." Bree lifted her gaze to Pamela and sighed. "Furthermore, the Priestess of the Spiral spoke the truth. Because she actively placed herself in conscious relationship with the Blade, Deirdre will be forever changed. She has connected with the vibration of the God, possibly even invoked It. That power will impact her, will interact with and reshape the song of her soul. Her soul's vibration will never be the same."

Bree glanced at her drum, resting on the floor beside her. Her eyebrows pulsed. "Approaching the Blade without proper training or mediation was disrespectful in the extreme. But removing the Blade from the men's village was sheer impudence. Clearly, she had enough skill to be in the Hallow's presence. She had to know there would be serious consequences."

She lifted her gaze and offered the sisters a wan smile. "The good news is the Hallow has been restored to Its rightful place. Positive, life-affirming flow should be restored and Pamela should recover."

"What if she doesn't?" Kat's voice pummeled the room.

"Then we have more Work to do."

Kat shook her head. "That isn't good enough."

"It is the best I can offer."

Kat's shoulders stiffened. With a sigh, she pushed herself to standing, then reached down to help her sister. "Come on. Let's get out of here."

From her seat on the meditation cushion, Pamela lifted her gaze and stared in rigid silence at her sister. To Bree's surprise, Kat stepped away from the dark-haired woman and sat back down without a word.

Pamela looked at Bree. "Whatever happens, I am grateful."

23

The bell over the front door spilled its soft chime through Fergus' office. Alone in the treatment room, Bree shook her head. The two sisters had departed, but the healing session was not quite complete. The circle she cast for the Work remained open.

After offering her thanks, Pamela had risen so abruptly she left Kat trailing three yards behind her all the way out the front door. Bree reached to stop the sisters, but the sudden change in her client left Bree speechless. In silent awe, she had watched the two women disappear.

Bree settled back onto the purple meditation cushion. Letting go of This World for the moment, she allowed her vision to soften. Bands of Otherworldly, opalescent light still shimmered along the periphery of the room, enfolding the space and sheltering the circle. Like spokes on a wheel, rays of brilliant, white light radiated outward from the circle's center to the opalescent blue edge. Shifting her gaze, Bree tracked those rays back to the center, to the candle flame still burning on the altar. Bathed in the flickering light, the crescent-shaped candle holder sparkled. Bree stared into the brilliance, then closed her eyes.

"Great Mother, Sacred Three, Mother Bríghid, thank you. Raven,

Bear, Stag and all my Allies, thank you. Spirits of the *Airds*—Center, West, South, East and North—thank you. For your shelter, your blessing, your Grace, this day and every day. For the wisdom shared, the healing offered and the gentle blessings, thank you."

"With gratitude," Bree drew her hands together, palms touching, before her heart, "I close this circle. This Work now done, Spirits who have held this circle," Bree pressed her hands away from her, opening her palms outward, "I release thee. Peace be upon you. Peace be upon me. Peace be upon this Working. Go in Peace and blessed be. *Sin é.*"

She bowed her head and touched the first three fingers of her right hand to her lips. Extending her hand outward, she released the kiss to the Otherworld.

Bree opened her eyes. The shimmering light of the journey circle was gone. In its place, the ordinary sage-green walls and earth-colored carpet of Fergus' clinic stretched around her.

Retuning her vision to This World, her gaze met that of the Kuan Yin statue standing opposite her. Golden-etched green and red light seeped from the goddess' heart. Slowly staining the wooden surface, it crept toward her extremities until it permeated the wooden image. Folding her hands over her own heart, Bree bowed in gratitude.

Blessed is the Mother. Blessed is the Mystery.

The candle flame on the altar flickered. Leaning forward, Bree gazed into the light.

Mother Bríghid, thank You for this flame. Thank You for the light of Your Love—in this room, in this circle, in this Working this day. Thank You for your healing Peace, now and always.

Bree wet the finger and thumb of her right hand upon her tongue, then held them to either side of the flame.

With Your gentle blessing, I offer this flame back to You.

Pressing her finger and thumb together, she extinguished the candle.

Sin é.

Three, thin wisps of white smoke curled above the wick. Stretching upward, they spiraled slowly around her hand, then vanished.

Bree reached to her left, toward the glass jar containing the water from Bríghid's sacred well. Once again, she dipped her three middle fingers into the water. Closing her eyes, she touched her fingers to her heart, her lips, her forehead. As the waters cleansed her, Bríghid's voice echoed through her.

"You are my Love. You are my Love. You are my Love."

Resting her hands over her heart, Bree bowed to the waters. *Blessed is the Mother. Blessed is the Mystery. Sin é.*

Opening her eyes, Bree grasped the clear-glass canning jar in her left hand and lifted it off the low, wooden altar. Settling back onto her cushion, she slid her right hand into her drum bag and pulled out the jar's metal top. She replaced the lid, gave it an extra turn to be sure it was sealed tightly, then returned the jar into the cloth bag.

Hand still inside, Bree reached into the bag's inner pocket. Her fingers shifted through the contents with the ease of familiarity and withdrew two tissues. She set one tissue upon her right knee and spread the second upon her left palm.

Leaning forward, she removed the ceramic bowl from the altar and emptied its long-cooled contents onto the tissue in her open hand. She set the ceramic bowl down on the carpet and wiped it clean with the second tissue. Then she placed the dirty tissue on the ashes in her left hand and folded both neatly into the first tissue. Her right hand again free, she picked up the ceramic bowl and slid it back into her bag. With her left, she tucked the remaining bundle into her jeans' pocket. She would offer the ashes, with her gratitude, to the earth once she was outside.

Footsteps padded on the soft carpet. As Bree slipped her *bodhrán* back into her drum bag, Fergus stepped into the open doorway and leaned against the jamb. He tilted his head and fiery red hair drifted down his shoulder.

"Well?"

Bree pulled the drum bag's zipper closed, then sat back on her heels. She looked at Pamela's empty meditation cushion. Images from the journey rippled through her, spilling questions with their wake.

What had protected Deirdre from the repercussions of stealing the Blade? Was the disappearance of the Blade the only reason for the discord between the men's and women's villages? And what prompted the Dagda to intervene on her behalf?

In Bree's inner vision, Pamela lifted her gaze and stared in rigid silence at her sister. As the ghostly image dissolved before her eyes, Bree wondered. What was the true nature of the relationship between the two sisters?

Remembering the fierceness of the otherwise wasting woman's reaction, Bree was certain the journey gifted a deep-level healing to Pamela and the other members of her Soul Spiral. But, here and now, would it be enough to restore Pamela's health?

Bree grabbed her drum bag. Shaking her head, she met Fergus' gaze. "The journey prompted almost as many questions as it answered."

"Is that a bad sign?"

She stood up and walked toward her friend. "Not exactly, but it is... unusual, especially for a healing session." Bree continued into the clinic waiting room and Fergus followed her. "The journey itself was complete, but..."

Bree slowed to a stop. Energy knotted and tugged in her belly. *Why not tell him?* She dropped her gaze to the drum bag in her hands and stared at the woven handles. *Because I so want to be wrong.*

"But, what?"

She turned to face him. "It just feels... unfinished." Fergus opened his mouth to speak but Bree silenced him. "Don't ask me how. I really cannot explain. Believe me, I wish I could."

"So," Fergus' eyes searched hers, "what now?"

She shrugged. "Give it time to integrate and see what happens."

Fergus nodded and took a step toward her. "Thanks for doing this." His hazel eyes caught and held hers. Warmth seeped through her as his fingers drifted slowly down her right arm to her wrist. "I mean it."

Bree stared at his fingers resting against her skin. Heat simmered beneath his touch and she shivered.

The bell spilled its soft chime through the waiting room.

Bree's head whirled toward the opening door to see a petite woman with long, dark braids entering the clinic. Fergus' fingers wrapped around her wrist and pressed gently. As she turned her head to face him, his hand dropped back to his side. His voice beside her was a whisper.

"It really is good to see you."

24

Bree tucked the cloth bag containing her drum and shamanic essentials securely in the back of her Jeep Wrangler. Her wrist still burned where Fergus had held her. He had touched her gently, but Bree could see the reddened outline of his fingers blazing upon her skin. Shifting forward, she gripped the steering wheel with both hands and exhaled forcefully.

She closed her eyes. In the darkness of her inner vision, the image of her still-packed suitcase hovered before her.

"No more running, Bree Nic Bhríde."

Bríghid's voice—feminine, ancient, loving—reverberated through Bree. She slumped in her seat and sighed.

Okay, Mother, we will do this Your way.

Bree opened her eyes. She lifted the lid on the lockbox nestled between the driver and front passenger seats and pulled out her telephone. At her touch, the screen winked to life.

3 Missed Calls: Caitlin MacLeod

Bree's eyes drifted up the screen. A small icon in the shape of a closed envelope gleamed in the upper left corner.

At least this time she left a message.

Tapping the icon with her finger, Bree waited as her telephone's voice messaging system engaged. A female, but not-quite-human, voice greeted her. "You have three new messages."

Bree pressed the needed numerical prompts and bypassed the mechanized voice. In its place, a familiar brogue filled her ear.

"Bree?" Caitlìn's soft burr spilled from the telephone. "Raven Child, are ye there?"

Her friend's voice disappeared in a riot of crackling and hissing. Then the recording ended.

Shivers snaked up Bree's spine as she followed the prompts and deleted the disrupted message. Lifting the telephone back to her ear, she tapped her toes nervously inside her boots. When Caitlìn's voice returned, tension clipped her friend's words and squeezed Bree's throat.

"Bree, I really must speak with ye. Urgently." Static snapped in the silence and sizzled along Bree's awareness. "Please, ring me. As soon as ye can."

What's happened?

Bree's fingers raced across the digital keypad. She held her breath and waited for the third voicemail message to play.

"Where are ye?" Strain etched her friend's voice, stretching it too high and too thin. "Bree, ye must know. I could no stop him. I tried, but..."

Her telephone chirruped, then fell silent. Furrowing her brow, Bree looked at the screen. The image of an empty battery flashed once, twice, then the entire screen went dark. She tapped it with her finger, but the screen remained blank.

"No, no, no!"

She pressed the power key. Nothing.

Bree stared at the dead telephone. "You've got to be joking."

She tucked the device between her knees and opened the lockbox beside her. Digging through its contents, she fished out her travel charger and plugged it into the USB port on the middle console. Grabbing her telephone, she connected it to the charger and dropped it into an empty cup holder.

She lifted her gaze to the silver Brìghid's cross hanging from her rearview mirror. The necklace and pendant were a gift from her cousine Rose, and Bree herself had transformed the simple ornament into an amulet. Blessed in the waters of Bríghid's well in Kildare and by the goddess Herself in the Otherworld, the silver cross became a Hallow. Bree kept it in her car always, to shelter her throughout her travels.

She wrapped her fingers around the talisman and closed her eyes.

Mother Bríghid, please, provided it does no harm, serves the Highest Good and honors all free will, I ask to know—is my kinswoman, Caitlin MacLeod in danger?

She held her breath, waiting, listening.

Power thrummed along her awareness, deep and broad, like the hum of bees within a hive. Sweetness washed through her mouth and spilled down her throat. *"She is well,"* the goddess' voice whispered, *"safe amidst the heather."*

Bree bowed her head and exhaled. *Thank you, Mother.* Releasing the talisman, she touched her fingertips to her heart, her lips, her forehead. *Blessed is the Mystery.*

Opening her eyes, she gazed gratefully at the small, silver cross.

Nothing to do now but wait.

She dug her car key out of her jeans' pocket and started the engine. As she pulled the seat belt across her shoulder, she glanced at the telephone. *How could it be dead?* She clicked the seat belt into place. *I charged it last night, didn't I?*

Bree shifted the Jeep into reverse and twisted to look behind her. Sunlight glinted through the rear compartment and, for a moment, a freeze-frame image of her bedroom nightstand hovered before her eyes. On its surface she could clearly see her telephone. *Only* her telephone.

Apparently not.

Bree's shoulders sagged. As the image faded from view, she chuckled.

Serves me right.

She backed out of her parking space and headed to her apartment. She was still laughing at her foolishness as she veered off

Delmar Boulevard, past the rod-iron, community gates and onto the winding streets of University Hills.

Bree completed the familiar turn onto her street, then slowed her approach. Leaning forward in her seat for a better view, she frowned. A steel-grey Ford Focus was parked in her driveway.

Whose car is that?

Caitlìn's voice rang through her. "I could no stop him. I tried, but..."

Bree shivered. "No..."

She steered into an open spot along the curb in front of her apartment. As the Jeep slowed to a stop, Bree glanced up the driveway.

Deep brown eyes met and held her gaze.

25

Bree's breath caught in her throat. Heat prickled her skin and stained her cheeks red. She knew she was staring, her mouth slowly gaping in surprise, but she could not look away.

The kilted man leaned against the driver's side of the rental car, one foot tucked up on the tire underneath him. The green and purple of the fine, MacLeod of Skye tartan gleamed in the afternoon sun. Deep, brown eyes watched her from under dark curls as a smile slowly spread across the man's face.

Hamish MacSween.

His deep brogue rose out of her memory. "Ye'd make a fine innswoman, Bree MacLeod."

They had worked together during her stay on the Isle of Skye, Scotland, running Heather House while Caitlìn was travelling in Cape Breton. Throughout her ten-week tenure, he had been more than helpful. He drove to Portree for groceries, ran loads of laundry, even conjured up extra beds when the B&B swelled to overflowing. Along the way, something had sparked between them.

"Bree!" The deep echo of raindrops pattered from Bree's memory. They sang a haunting counterpoint to Hamish's distraught cry. In her inner vision, Hamish's face pressed against her rain-streaked car window as his hands rested upon the glass. Water spilled down his curls but his eyes never left her own. Concern etching his features, he mouthed, "Are ye all right?"

Bree blinked and let the memory fade from view. Her body trembled. Then and now, she had not expected him to care enough to come and find her.

A ghostly caress shivered along her skin and Bree closed her eyes. His hands had glided slowly up her arms and drawn her closer to him. On their one and only date, Bree had stood shaking in his arms, her forehead resting against his chest. He never pressed her. Not that night nor through the remaining days they had worked side by side.

Heat rushed from her core. Much to her surprise, she had enjoyed standing in his arms. But she walked away unable to embrace anything more.

From the cup holder beside her seat, her telephone chimed back to life.

Bree dropped her gaze and stared at the new message icon glowing on the reanimated screen. *At least Caitlin tried to warn me.*

As she turned off the Jeep's engine, her gaze drifted back to the man now crossing her front yard. The MacLeod of Skye tartan swayed playfully above muscular knees and leather walking shoes.

Bree forced herself to look away. She focused instead on gathering her drum bag from the back seat. *Breathe. Just breathe.* Setting the bag on the passenger seat, she unplugged her telephone and slid it into the bag's front pocket. Grabbing the cloth handles, she turned and reached for her door. It was already open.

Hamish stood before her. Bunched in his right hand, a dozen red roses peeked out above cream-colored paper.

Dark eyes twinkling, he sought and held her eyes. "I suppose coffee might hae been a better choice, but..." He looked down at the flowers, then extended them toward her. "For ye."

26

"Hamish," Bree shook her head and hopped out of her Jeep. "What are you doing here?"

His smile faded. "Are ye no happy tae see me?"

She stood looking at him. *Am I?*

Heat shivered under her skin. With a soft sigh, she smiled. "Of course I am. It's just... well... a bit... unexpected."

Nodding, he dropped his head and rocked onto his heels. He lifted his gaze and his brown eyes peered out at her, twinkling between the red roses and his dark curls. "Are ye angry wi' me?"

Bree chuckled despite herself. *Mischievous laddie.*

Black hair spilled down her shoulders as she shook her head. "No, just... surprised."

A smile spread slowly across his face. "Right, then..." He lifted the bouquet up closer to his chin.

Bree laughed. "I guess you'd better come in."

He stood beaming at her as she stepped out of the way of the car door. After pushing it closed, he followed her across the lawn and up the front walkway.

Bree slid the key into the lock on the front door of her apartment. Behind her, Hamish joined her on the front step. He was so close.

Gentle warmth radiated from his body. Spilling down her back and shoulders, it enfolded her. Like an embrace, it wrapped around her, drew her nearer.

She reached for the doorknob and he took a step closer. His breath drifted, soft and sensual, down her neck. Heat rushed through her body, singeing her cheeks, and she willed her breathing to slow. As she pushed the door open, his arm reached around her. His shoulder against hers, his broad hand pressed and held the door open.

His chin brushed against her ear. "M'lady."

Bree shivered. With a muttered, "Thanks," she stepped into the foyer and hurried to the dining room table.

Breathe. Just breathe.

She placed her drum bag on the table, then turned to face Hamish. He stood a few feet away from her, roses outstretched before him. His eyes watched her, dark and brooding.

Bree smiled warmly and took the bouquet from his hand. Bending close enough to touch her nose to the flowers, she inhaled their silky perfume. Soft and tender, rosy-pink light shimmered through her.

"*Tapadh leat*...Thanks, Hamish." She raised her eyes to his. "They are lovely."

He stepped closer, his eyes locked on her face. He reached for the bouquet, removed it from her hands and set it on the table. Stepping closer still, he took her hands in his.

"I had tae see ye."

His brown eyes searched hers. Still holding her hands, he stretched the fingers of his right hand to caress her hair. Twining a strand through his fingers, he stepped even closer.

"I know..." He dropped his gaze and swallowed. "I know we may never be."

"Hamish..." Bree's voice was a whisper.

His dark curls shook with his head. "No, lass. Please," he lifted his eyes to hers. "Lemme speak."

Bree closed her mouth and nodded.

"Right." He drew a slow breath and his eyes searched hers. "While I know *this*," he pressed her hands with his, "may never be—I'm your man."

Hamish stood there, looking at her, his eyes shimmering.

"I cannae stop thinking about ye. I drive by the tor and look for your car. I see your black hair dancing in the wind, then turn to see its no you. In the post office, I hear your laugh but you're no there." He shook his head. "You're with me, wherever I go." He dropped his gaze and sighed. "And, the thing is... well..." He looked up at her from under lowered eyelids. "I like it." A slow smile spread across his face as his eyes held her own. "Nay... I love it."

A thick strand of Bree's hair slipped down, concealing the left side of her face. Hamish reached up and gently swept it back behind her ear. His fingertips brushed her cheek and Bree's breath caught in her throat.

"So, ye see, I had tae come. If only tae be near ye. Een for just a little while."

Bree dropped her gaze to her right hand, still resting in his. She shivered. *Am I truly ready? Can I really try again?*

He had always been so kind and caring with her. She had replayed their date in the grove so many times in her mind and she had to admit—she truly wished it could have ended differently. But, while the attraction between them was undeniable, could she open her heart to Love with a man?

In her inner vision, ten, pale mounds rose and fell in rapid succession as the Dagda's voice rumbled through her from the Otherworld. *"Friends?"*

She lifted her gaze. Hamish's deep brown eyes watching her, encouraged her.

The soft, earthy scent of pinesap filled her nose. Bree leaned toward him. She wanted to reach out, but hesitated. Instead, she nodded. "Where are you staying?"

Hamish inhaled slowly and took a step back, releasing her hand. "The Starlight."

"A fun choice. But, it's rather urban." She tilted her head. "Are you sure you wouldn't prefer something a bit quieter?" Bree cast her gaze down the hallway. She gestured with her left hand at the open door to her guestroom. "It's not as cozy as Heather House, but you'd be very welcome."

Following her gaze, Hamish shook his head. "No, lass. I came on me own and I'll no trespass more. But," he lifted hopeful eyes, "I'm in room 309, if ye care for a bit of company."

He reached out and took her hand in his. Eyes locked upon hers, he lifted her hand to his lips and kissed it. Then, releasing her hand, he turned and headed to the front door.

"Hamish."

He stood facing the closed door, his hand gripping the doorknob. Bree crossed the foyer and stopped a few paces behind him.

"The roses are beautiful. Thank you."

Without turning, he nodded, dark curls spilling.

Bree reached out, slid the fingertips of her right hand down the middle of his back. Over his left shoulder, his brown eyes met hers.

"It *is* lovely to see you."

Kilt swaying gently, he released the doorknob and turned to face her. His hands reached for hers, slid up her arms to rest above her elbows. He took a step closer, then waited.

Bree shivered. Her heart pounded in her chest but she could not move. Not even as he turned and walked out her front door.

27

I've let him go... again. Bree stared at the closed front door of her apartment. *Is that really what I want?* She dropped her gaze to the floor. *How? How do I move on?*

From the corner of her eye, she could see her suitcase, packed and waiting for her. She took a step closer and let her fingers drift across its leather handle. The solid, stone walls and sloped thatching of her cottage in Ireland filled her inner vision.

Ireland... Cill Dara... refuge...

She closed her eyes and let her fingers fall from the suitcase. Her hand settled back to her side.

Mother Bríghid is right. That won't solve anything.

Opening her eyes, she turned away from her suitcase and walked toward the dining room table. The red roses remained where Hamish had left them. Bundled in their cream-colored paper, they lay waiting for her. Sighing deeply, she picked up the bouquet and headed down the hall.

The broad heels of her boots reverberated against the oakwood floor. Echoing like a heartbeat through the hallway, the sound pounded through Bree. The door on the left at the far end of the hallway pulled at her. Lifting her gaze, her eyes traced the spiraling lines of the tricele she herself had painted on the wood.

She slowed before the open doorway to the kitchen. As her eyes lingered on the tricele, the image pulsed with the heartbeat still thrumming in her ears. She stood staring at the swirling dance, then turned and walked into the kitchen.

The heartbeat throbbed through her.

She pulled a vase out of the cupboard under the sink. Opening the faucet, she placed the etched, glass container under the running water. Spirals and triceles pulsed within the flowing stream, streaking the water black, red and white. A deep toning spilled from the floor, up her legs and into her pelvis.

She closed the faucet and set the vase on the counter. She untied the cream-colored, cloth ribbon, pulled the roses out of the wrapping paper and lowered the stems into the vase. All while the deep tone ached its way from her pelvis toward her heart.

Her whole body vibrated. Hands again free, she leaned them against the counter and exhaled.

Leaving everything in the kitchen, she stepped back into the hallway and looked to her left, at the door to her sanctuary. The painted tricele swirled before her, releasing small black, red and white spirals to cascade through the hallway. They whirled around her, aching with the reverberating beat as the toning resounded through her heart.

A white spiral danced before her eyes. Shimmering with each pulsation, it drifted away from her and down the hallway. Unable to look away, Bree watched it disappear beyond the doorway to the bedroom.

Our bedroom.

Memories throbbed through her... Gwen laughing, toboggan in hand and bundled against the falling snow as she dragged Bree up Art Hill in Forest Park... Gwen's curly, red hair spilling down Bree's shoulder as they sipped coffee under their favorite oak tree... Gwen cooking dinner, her hips swaying as her slightly off-pitch voice echoed through their kitchen... those same hips nestled against

Bree as she curled her body around Gwen's before drifting into sleep...

Bree closed her eyes.

Hamish's brown eyes filled her inner vision as he lifted her hand to his lips. "M'Lady..." his voice whispered in her ear, his chin brushing her cheek.

Bree's body shook.

The deep sound droned in her head. Tones stretched and blended, harmonizing into a voice. An Otherworldly voice, calling from her childhood, from a past Bree thought she had forgotten.

"Love is the fundamental vibration." Bríghid's voice reverberated through her. *"Energy, life, everything is created in Love, pulsates with Love and is Love in manifestation."*

Bree was a novice again, a young girl standing alone in her family grove in Seattle. In her small hands she held a glass globe in which burned a solitary candle, the sole illumination for the night's Working.

The goddess gestured toward the flickering flame. As Bree dropped her gaze to the light, it swelled and morphed into a single flame burning in an ancient, earthen brazier. Gazing into that fire, the world opened before Bree. The faces of loved ones and strangers alike rippled into and out of view. She witnessed the earth in its becoming, even the cosmos spiraling in its endless dance.

Her young self had gaped in awe as Bríghid's voice resounded. *"Everything is sacred, born of the Lovemaking of the Mother, the Father and the Creator, of the sacred fire of life."*

The deep tone ached through Bree's adult body, throbbing with the heartbeat along every nerve.

"The Mother... the Chalice." Bríghid's voice rang in haunting counterpoint as that ancient brazier still burned in Bree's inner vision. *"The Father... the Blade. The Creator... the Loving... the Flame."*

The fire flickered, then rushed outward and scattered in all directions before coalescing into starry pinpoints. A smile, tender and inviting, flashed out of that light and spread across a woman's face. Ancient and ageless, the Goddess drew her lover's face to hers.

"Mo ghrá... My Love..." the God's voice, deep and rumbling, tumbled through Bree as she watched lips welcome lips.

Heat seared along her skin. Her heart racing in her chest, Bree struggled to slow her breathing as, all around her, the heartbeat thundered—*Love, Love, Love.*

"Come home, Bree Nic Bhríde." Bríghid's voice called through the throbbing song. *"Come home to Love."*

Bree opened her eyes. Shivering, she turned and strode back toward the front door. She grabbed her keys off the dining room table, crossed the foyer and reached for the front door. Doorknob in hand, she looked at the couch and loveseat.

Empty, like our apartment.

My apartment.

She stepped out the front door and pulled it closed behind her.

28

"Here you go, love." Chelle slid a pint of cider onto the bar next to the heaping basket of homemade potato crisps in front of Bree.

As Chelle leaned toward her, Bree let her gaze drift—from the cropped and red-tipped, brown hair, along the gentle curve of Chelle's cheek and down the smooth swell of her breasts. Soft and tender, rosy-pink light shimmered through Bree.

Chelle tilted her head and smiled. "Anything else?"

Finding the woman's eyes, Bree returned the smile. "Maybe later. Can I let you know?"

Chelle winked. "Anytime you're ready."

Bree leaned forward and rested her elbow on the bar. She propped her chin on her hand. "You really are so good to me."

"Nothing easier, hon." Chelle chuckled softly. With a quick nod, she rose and walked back toward the kitchen.

Bree watched Chelle's swaying hips disappear through the wooden archway. Eyes locked on the spot where the woman had disappeared, Bree reached for her pint of cider.

What am I doing?

Bree had found Chelle attractive from the start. Somehow she took to flirting with the woman, something Chelle appeared to enjoy and always returned in kind. Just who had initiated it, Bree could not remember now. Once, Bree asked Gwen if their flirting bothered her. Gwen just shook her head and replied, "Although, I sometimes wonder if you two used to be lovers." But Gwen knew better. She had been in Bree's life long before Chelle first appeared at the Gráinne Uaile.

Is this what I want?

Bree shifted her gaze back to the bar and swallowed a mouthful of cider.

This is what I know.

The reply came unbidden from deep within her. Bree straightened and set her cider down on the bar.

"Could it be time to learn something more?" The voice of Emily, her aunt and foster-mother, echoed through Bree.

Heart pounding, Bree closed her eyes.

Golden light shimmered behind her eyelids, rippling and undulating like waves on a pond. Bree's Salmon Ally lifted its head out of those waters and hovered before her. Its copper tail swayed side to side and its rounded eyes closed. When they opened again, a familiar pair of hazel eyes gazed back at Bree. Otherworldly bright, her aunt stared at her.

"I was afraid of drowning in that Love."

Bree gasped. Six months ago her aunt had spoken those words to her in a journey. From the depths of a coma—and with Bree by her side—Emily had reached to embrace Love as her doorway back to physical life.

"I was afraid." Emily shook her head. *"But no more."*

Bree's thigh burned. Opening her eyes, she reached into her pocket. She pulled out the stone carving of the fleur-de-lys and stared at it. No blood spilled from it today, but she could still see the Otherworldly cracks stretching through the central petal. As she ran her thumb over the carved image, tears pooled in her eyes.

Warmth spread across her left shoulder and slid slowly down the center of her back. Blinking away tears, Bree looked up into Chelle's green eyes. The woman slipped her arm around Bree's waist and drew Bree close.

"You okay?"

For a heartbeat, maybe two, Bree let herself lean into Chelle's warmth. Then, forcing a smile, she nodded.

Chelle sat down in the high barchair beside Bree. "You miss her."

Yes, Bree sighed inwardly. *I do miss Gwen. But is that all this really is?* She furrowed her brow. *Am I just clinging to Gwen? Is that why I cannot seem to move on? Or is Emily right? Am I afraid of what I might be becoming?*

A lump filled Bree's throat. As she struggled to swallow it, a tear spilled down her cheek. Chelle reached up and wiped it away tenderly. Her eyes caught Bree's.

"I'm off in an hour. Why don't you tell me about it then?"

29

Sunlight sparkled through Bree's eyelids. Pressing her eyes more tightly closed, she rolled onto her right side and snuggled her head into the pillow beneath her. Her forehead touched something soft and warm.

Someone sighed.

Bree opened her eyes. Chelle's bare shoulder peeked enticingly out from under the tangerine-orange, cotton sheet draped across her sleeping form.

"You are full of surprises today."

Bree lifted her head. Gwen sat on the far edge of the queen-sized bed. A smirk stretching across her face, she stared at Chelle, then shifted her gaze to Bree.

"Not quite the bed I expected to find you in this morning." Red curls shook with Gwen's head as she laughed. *"Shows you how much I know."*

Bree lowered her head onto the pillow. Beside her, Chelle's breathing flowed with the slow, steady rhythm of deep sleep. Bree let her eyes drift across the smooth skin of the woman's back once more, then rolled over and slid gently out of the bed. She gathered her things from the floor and slipped quietly into her clothes. As she buttoned up her black overshirt, she gazed at the sleeping woman.

Gwen chuckled. *"You missed one."*

Bree glared at Gwen.

The corners of her mouth twitching against a smirk, Gwen shrugged. *"What?"*

Bree fixed her buttons and ran her fingers through her sleep-tossed hair. Shooing Gwen with her hands, she crossed to the far side of the bed. She bent over Chelle's sleeping form and kissed the exposed shoulder tenderly. With a soft smile, she rose and turned toward the bedroom door.

Gwen leaned against the doorjamb, her arms folded across her chest. Her ghostly form filled the doorway.

Bree stopped in front of her and stared.

Gwen leaned forward. *"Are you really just going to leave?"*

Bree pressed her hands to her hips. When Gwen remained standing there, Bree mouthed, "MOVE!"

Gwen's mouth gaped. She shook her head and stepped to the side. *"I'm only trying to help, you know."*

Bree stepped through the open doorway and heaved a sigh. She scanned the room and spotted her black fleece jacket draped across the back of the couch. Slipping her arms into the sleeves, she crossed to the center of the room and shuffled through the magazines and papers scattered on the coffee table. Half-hidden beneath a new edition of *St. Louis Foodies*, she found an empty envelope and a pen.

She crouched beside the table, pulled the cap off the pen, then paused.

"Better make it good."

Bree slanted her eyes up at Gwen. Shaking her head, she bent over the envelope. "A beautiful morning to a beautiful lady." Her distinctive block letters stretched across the white paper. "Thanks... for everything—Bree."

She slid the cap back onto the pen and set it on the table. Rising from her crouch, she looked at the note—just one more bit of paper on a crowded coffee table. *She'll never see it there.*

Bree picked up the note and looked around the room. Tapping the paper against her right palm, she wondered where would be the best place to leave it. Her gaze drifted to the bedroom and Bree smiled.

She tip-toed alongside the bed and placed the note on the nightstand, next to Chelle's telephone.

Bree stood watching Chelle sleep. *Lovely,* Bree smiled. *Truly lovely.* She pressed her right fingertips to her lips and blew the sleeping woman a kiss. She backed softly away from the bed just as Gwen entered the room and leaned over the nightstand. With a quick grin, Bree turned and headed back into the living room.

She found her square-toed boots strewn across the floor just inside the front door. As Bree bent over and pulled them on, Gwen appeared before her. Hands upon her hips, Gwen stared stiffly at Bree. Then a grin crept across her face.

"That was my line."

30

Bree stared at the willow tree before her. Its long limbs waved in the gentle breeze as it whispered. *"Welcome back, Bree Nic Bhríde."*

Her Jeep Wrangler idled in her favorite parking spot at the Sophia Center. Once again she had arrived there without intending to do so. Gripping the steering wheel until her knuckles blanched, Bree dropped her head between her hands.

"What am I doing here?'

"Well, that depends."

Bree rolled her forehead along the steering wheel and looked toward the Otherworldly voice. Her dead mother, Bríde, sat in the Jeep's passenger seat.

"Do you mean—" her mother gestured to the rolling green space around her, *"what are you doing here, in this parking lot? Or,"* she leaned sideways and placed her right hand upon Bree's heart, *"what are you doing... here?"*

Bree sat back in the driver's seat and stared at her mother. She threw her hands into the air and shook her head. "Either. Both."

"Running away again."

Bree's head snapped up and she glared at her mother.

"It's the truth." Bríde's gaze softened. *"What is it, child? Why do you*

continue to refuse the Love your heart so clearly feels?"

Beyond her mother's ghostly form, Bree could see the wooden trellis that marked the entrance to the Center's labyrinth. Like her family grove in Seattle and Bríghid's Enclosure in Kildare, this had always been a place of Truth, refuge and discovery for Bree. So why was she so reluctant to answer?

"What are you so afraid of?"

Tears welled in Bree's eyes and she dropped her gaze.

"Very well." Bríde sighed and leaned back in the passenger seat. *"If you cannot speak of it with me, perhaps you need to hear it from another."*

Bree frowned. Another?

"What do you mean?" Bree looked up but the passenger seat was empty. "Mother?"

The bouncing notes of an Irish jig echoed through the Jeep. Bree pulled the vibrating telephone out of her jeans' pocket and Emily's familiar, hazel eyes gazed back at her from the glowing screen. Bree touched the green, answer icon and lifted the telephone to her ear.

"Foster-mother?"

"Raven Child!" Concern edged her aunt's voice. "What is it? What's wrong?"

Bree frowned. "Wrong?"

Emily huffed. "The ravens have been clamoring at me for the past half hour. Now, I have a vision of you in tears." She paused. "What ever is the matter, *a stór*?"

Bree hesitated. *What do I say? How can I ask her?* She took a deep breath. "How is Ciara?"

"Ciara?" A wave of surprise buffeted Bree. "She is well."

Bree nibbled her lip. "And, you are happy... with her?"

"Very." Her aunt's voice softened. "Bree, I have no regrets, if that is what you are asking."

Bree closed her eyes. "It's just... I..."

"You've met someone."

"A man." Bree sighed. "How... How can I be sure it isn't just grief? Or some strange way of preserving my love for Gwen?" Opening her eyes, she stared at the willow tree before her. "How can I throw away everything I know, everything I have been—upset my entire world—for something that might not even last?"

Silence settled around Bree. *There, I've said it. I've acknowledged it to another person. And the Sacred is always listening.* Her body trembled.

"Foster-daughter," tenderness enfolded Bree with Emily's voice, "what do you feel when he touches you?"

Heat flashed through Bree's skin. "Fire."

"Everything is sacred, born of the Lovemaking of the Mother, the Father and the Creator, of the sacred fire of life." Bríghid's voice resounded through Bree's body as the deep drone of a heartbeat thrummed along her nerves. *"The Mother... the Chalice. The Father... the Blade. The Creator... the Loving... the Flame."*

Bree closed her eyes.

Firelight flickered in her inner vision, then rushed outward and scattered in all directions before coalescing into starry pinpoints. A smile, tender and inviting, flashed out of that light and spread across a woman's face. Ancient and ageless, the Goddess drew her lover's face to hers. *"Mo ghrá... My love..."* the God's voice, deep and rumbling, tumbled through Bree as she watched lips welcome lips.

"The sacred flame of Creation." Emily sighed. "So, that isn't the problem."

Bree shivered. "No."

"Then, what is? Child, what are you afraid of?"

Images from her past kaleidoscoped from Bree's memory... her uncle's face, eyes closed in prayer and hovering a breath's edge from her own, his hands painfully pressing a cross into her forehead as water dripped down her face... Bree and Amber, her first girlfriend, pressed back to back, tensed to fight the men slowly surrounding them... hands forcing Bree's mouth open as her uncle poured something cold and sour down her throat... lolling, beaten and drugged, in her uncle's arms as—against her will—he had her committed...

Bree shuddered. "Foster-mother, I chose this way of life, this way of Loving. I nearly died for it. If... if this is not who I am, then... what was it all for?"

The droning heartbeat pulsed through her. "*Love, Love, Love,*" it sang.

"That, *a stór*, I do not know." Emily's voice was tender. "But I do know this, now more than ever. Love is the fundamental vibration of life."

"I believe that, too."

"Good." Emily paused. "Do you also believe, as our tradition teaches, that all life emerges out of Love, that all life *is* Love in manifestation? That everything is a manifestation of Love, a manifestation of the Sacred Love-Making and, therefore, is equally Sacred? That Masculine, Feminine, Creative are all equally Sacred, equally Love-filled and equally Love?"

Bree's voice was a whisper. "You know I do."

"Then, you must also agree that as Love is the fundamental vibration, *Loving* is a sacred act—is *the* sacred act—in *all* of its manifestations."

"Yes."

"Then why does it matter if it is a woman or a man who sets the song of Love to singing within you? In *all* its manifestations, Foster-daughter." Emily took a breath. "Let me ask it another way. Knowing and believing all of this, how could you dare to throw away the Sacred's gift of Love and the Grace that Love might awaken within you?"

"You make it sound so easy."

"Do I?" Emily sighed. "We all have our places of resistance. You and the Goddess know just how difficult this was for me."

Bree blinked. An image of her aunt, withered and unconscious, flashed before her. The pale, wispy form seemed to seep away before Bree's eyes, slowly dissolving into the piercing white of hospital sheets.

"What do your Allies say about this?"

Bree stared at the woven trellis that marked the entrance to the Center's labyrinth. "I haven't asked them."

"Maybe it's time you did."

31

Bree pushed the front door of her apartment closed. After locking it behind her, she bent down and pulled off her boots. As she rose to standing, her gaze settled on the empty couch and love seat.

Bree turned her back to the vacant living room. Her woolen socks padding softly against the oakwood floor, she crossed toward the dining room table. She pulled her telephone out of her jeans' pocket and, without stopping, dumped it, and her keys, onto the wooden surface. Then she turned and headed down the hall.

The tricele on her sanctuary door gleamed, illuminated in a drifting ray of sunshine. Her feet slowed to a standstill and she stood, waiting. No heartbeat thrummed around her now. The spiraling image remained unmoving before her, just ordinary paint and wood.

Sunlight glinted across the left side of her face. Squinting against the glare, she turned her head and the kitchen opened before her. The bouquet of roses from Hamish blazed a deep, lustrous red in the noon-hour light.

Emily's voice echoed through her. *"What do you feel when he touches you?"*

Heat singed Bree's skin. Her face reddened and her heart pounded within her chest. "Fire," she whispered.

"*What do your Allies say about this?*"

Bree lowered her chin and stared at the floor. *She's right. It's time to ask.* Slowly, she raised her head and her eyes traced the tricele. *It's time to know how to move on.*

She nodded once, then walked down the hallway. Turning left into her sanctuary, Bree closed the door behind her.

The room looked just as she remembered. Wooden bookcases lined the perimeter, their shelves crammed to overflowing with books, stones from the sacred places dear to her, and images of the goddess Bríghid she had found in her travels and studies. In the east, a single, white candle rested atop a large, broad, flat stone.

Bree smiled. She remembered carrying that stone back with her from Ireland years ago. She first encountered it on the property she inherited from her mother. The perfect altar stone for her sanctuary, she asked the Spirit of the stone for its permission to bring it with her to America. Too heavy to check as cargo—and too precious to entrust to baggage—Bree had lugged it through connection after connection, tucking it under the seat in front of her on each flight. She could not remember ever feeling so safe on an airplane, her feet resting on a stone twice hallowed, blessed as it was by three goddesses, Bríghid, Ériu and Dána.

Her eyes drifted to the *bodhrán* standing on its edge just to the left of the altar stone. Slightly larger than the drum she used during her session with Pamela, this drum accompanied Bree on her personal journeys and no others. Dancing crimson-orange, an image of the Sacred Flame blazed across its surface.

Bree grinned at the drum. "Hello, old friend." She stepped forward and lifted it tenderly. "*Beannachtaí agus síocháin duit...*" she whispered into the hide, "Blessings and peace be upon you."

The drum trembled in her hands, then warmth enfolded her, spreading around her like the arms of a lover or an old friend. "*Fáilte abhaile...*" the spirit of the drum whispered, "*Welcome home.*"

Bree wrapped her arms around the frame and pressed the hide to her chest. Sorrow welled from the depths of her soul. *How could I have walked away from this? Denied this part of me?* She fought back a sob. *I have been away too long.*

She kissed the arching frame. "*Tá brón orm…* I am sorry. I should not have left you."

"*Ní hea…Nay…*" warmth hugged her. "*You needed time to grieve.*"

Bree rested her cheek upon the cool wood.

"*Whenever you are ready, we are still here…*"

A tear spilled down Bree's cheek and she closed her eyes. "*Go raibh mille maith agaibh…* Thank you."

Once again, she kissed the top of the drum, then returned it to its spot beside the altar. She dug the meditation mat and cushion she used for journeys out of the closet and returned them to their usual place in the center of the room. She remembered tucking them away for safe-keeping before she left for Ireland. "No reason to sit around out there, gathering dust," she had muttered to the items as she settled them in the closet. Now, her fingers tingled at their touch. Glee rushed up her arms and into her chest, and she actually laughed out loud.

Still chuckling softly, she retrieved the lighter from the nearest bookshelf and knelt before the altar. Bowing her head, Bree lit the candle.

"Mother Bríghid, bless this flame. Let this flame shine the light of your Love into this room, this journey, this Working this day. Shelter, support and imbue this Working with your healing Peace. *Sin é.*"

Brilliant white light flashed, radiating outward from the center of the candle flame and spilling through the room to enfold Bree in a shimmering circle. Smiling softly, Bree closed her eyes.

"Peace be in this space… Peace be in this circle…" The words flowed effortlessly, like the radiance streaming to fill the room. "Peace be in this Working…"

Opalescent light shimmered in her inner vision. As tears pooled in her eyes, the edges of her awareness slowly dissolved and she slipped into the Otherworld.

32

Bree stands in darkness. Feet bare upon the earth, she shivers as a cool breeze tosses her hair. She draws her woolen cloak around her and lifts her gaze to the night sky.

No moon greets her. The sky stretches dark in all directions, like the landscape around her.

Burning wood crackles and snaps behind her. Startled, she turns toward the sound and inhales sharply. In the distance, a single flame blazes into the night.

"Are you ready?"

Bree lowers her chin and looks toward the voice. Her Bear Ally sits before her, dark eyes fixed on Bree. Lifting her right hand to her heart, Bree bows her head in greeting.

"Síocháin duit... Peace be upon you..." Head bowed, Bree waits for her Ally's response.

"Peace be between us," Bear says without moving.

Bree lifts her eyes to meet those of her Ally and they finish the ritual greeting together. "Now and through all time."

Silence settles between them. Only the cracking and snapping of the burning wood disturbs the night.

Bear lifts her snout and tilts her head. "What brings you here, Raven Child?"

Bree glances at the fire burning in the distance, then takes a step toward her Ally. "Bear, I come with a question for myself."

Bear's eyes glisten despite the darkness. "Then ask it."

Nodding, Bree takes a deep breath. "How do I move on from here? After everything that has been, how may I embrace life and Loving again?"

Bear stares at Bree. Slowly, her Ally rises to all fours. "Come," Bear turns toward the fire. Glancing back at Bree, she chuffs. "Follow me closely."

Bree walks behind her Ally. Keeping no more than two paces between them, Bree places her feet carefully in Bear's round paw prints. In her mind's eye, she can see those same paw prints disappearing into the earth behind her.

As they draw near the fire, it hisses and snaps, then spits a single, long flare into the night. Separated from the blaze, that single flame stretches and twists until the curving shape of a woman burns before Bree. Fiery eyes lock upon Bree and the blazing goddess walks toward her.

Bree falls to her knees.

Her training screams within her, urging Bree to bow in honoring. But she cannot look away.

The fiery eyes shimmer. Frozen before them, Bree watches their crimson-orange glare slowly cool to silvery white. Glittering like stars, those eyes wash Bree in brilliance to the depths of her soul.

With a final flash, the flame melts into the night. In its place, a woman —ancient, yet youthful—stands before Bree.

"Beannachtaí, mo Ghrá ...Blessings, my Love..."

The goddess Brighid gleams beneath the plain, white scarf draped over her head. With a smile, she steps forward and kisses Bree's forehead. Fiery light pours through Bree, cascading downward to flood the depths of her being. Without looking, Bree knows—numinous, white light streams from her every pore.

Bree vibrates, mind body and soul. Bathed in a love so pure, so compassionate, so complete, she trembles. Closing her eyes, she bows in honoring... "Mother Brighid."

Warmth pools atop her head, then spills slowly down her spine. Bree opens her eyes and sees the goddess' hand resting upon her head.

"What brings you here, mo Ghrá... my Love?"

Bree rises to her knees. "How do I move on from here? After everything that has been, how may I embrace life and Loving again?"

Bríghid gestures to her right. Bree shifts her gaze and sees a small blade, a skean dubh, sheathed and resting upon the flat surface of a large stone. Beside it stands the ceramic stem of a chalice. Bree frowns. The cauldron portion of the chalice is missing. All around the stem, small, earthen shards lie strewn, half hidden in the shadows drifting across the stone.

She stares at the items on the stone. The image of a chalice shattering flashes through her. Blinking back tears, Bree stifles a gasp. The stem and pieces are what remain of the broken chalice.

"Do you know the story of the Cup of Truth?"

Bríghid's voice washes over Bree and she shivers. Unable to shift her eyes from the shards flickering in the firelight, Bree shakes her head.

"It is a gift of Manannán mac Lir. When a falsehood is spoken over it, the Cup shatters. To restore the Cup to wholeness, a truth must then be spoken over the pieces."

Bríghid pauses. As Bree stares at the ceramic bits strewn across the stone, the hissing fire fills her ears.

"These are the Chalice and Blade of your life," the goddess continues. "As you can see, the Chalice lies in pieces. Like the Cup of Truth, a falsehood has shattered it. To move forward from here, you must speak the truth that repairs it."

Bree lifts her gaze. "What truth restores it to wholeness?"

Bríghid's eyes blaze in the darkness. "Speak the answer to this question over the stem and pieces: What do you choose—the dead or the living?"

Bree stares at the goddess.

"Remember," Bríghid leans toward her, "only the truth will restore the Chalice."

Bree nods. She turns toward the stone. Her Bear Ally sits beside it, dark eyes watching Bree. As Bree steps close enough to the stone to lean over it, a sob gasps from her chest.

"I choose the living."

Opalescent light shimmers around the edges of each shard. One by one the pieces begin to quiver upon the stone. As the shaking grows in intensity, they slide and jump until, with a blazing flash of brilliant bluish-purple light, they fly together. Bree blinks. The Chalice stands upon the stone, fully restored to wholeness.

The chalice shimmers in the night. Radiant light rises out of the restored cauldron. Bree leans forward and peers inside it. An opalescent liquid flows within the bowl.

A gleaming hand grasps the chalice and lifts it off the stone. As Bree's eyes track the rising chalice, they meet those of the goddess.

Brighid extends the restored cup to Bree. "Drink, mo Ghrá... my Love. Receive the three healing drops to restore you."

With shaking hands, Bree reaches out and receives the Chalice from the mother of her lineage. As her fingers touch the ancient clay, a deep toning aches up her legs and into her heart. The toning floods into her head and a pulsing heartbeat throbs through her.

Bree's heart pounds. The closer the Chalice comes to her, the brighter the liquid inside glows. With both hands wrapped around the archaic stem, she lifts the gleaming cup to her lips. To her surprise, the clay is cool against her skin. She had expected it to be warm.

She tilts the cup toward her and swallows... once, twice, three times. Opalescent light cascades through her. Crashing in waves, bluish-purple light floods her vision and she extends the Chalice toward the goddess. Brighid smiles and, with a blinding flash, Bree dissolves into whiteness.

33

Bree's heart pounded. Eyes closed to the room around her, she sat slumped over the *bodhrán* still grasped in her left hand. Bluish-white light danced in her inner vision and a slightly sweet taste spilled through her mouth. Body trembling, she swallowed.

I choose the living.

Her voice echoed through her. In her ears, the Sacred Flame still snapped and crackled. She knew the Flame had heard her, was listening to her still. She had spoken an oath—in the Otherworld, before the goddess Bríghid and her Bear Ally, and with the Sacred Flame as witness. She would be held accountable.

The Sacred is always listening.

"In the sacred dance of co-creation, human beings hold the gift of choice..." Emily's voice drifted to Bree from her childhood.

Bree shuddered. Opalescent light washed through her. Her body rippled once, twice, three times, then lost its cohesion. Shimmering life force rushed within her inner vision, cascading downward like a waterfall. Bree fell with those running waters, tumbling end over end. As those waters pooled, Bree was a girl again. She sat on Emily's couch, her feet dangling in home-woven wool socks. Her cousine Rose beside her, Bree looked up into her aunt's loving face.

"As souls, we enter every lifetime with a purpose—a list of experiences to be had, energies to cultivate, tasks to complete. Each soul is free to choose how it walks through a given lifetime—how it denies, acknowledges or completes its purpose. For only a soul can know what choice upholds its purpose, maintains its integrity and cultivates authenticity. And every soul has the right to create its own experience.

"Choice is a sacred right, and a soul's choice *must* be honored."

Bree's soul rushed upward, rising to fill her adult form, still slumped over her drum. Fire hissing in her ears, Bree inhaled slowly, pulling her awareness back into This World. That sweet taste flowed into her mouth and Bree swallowed.

How many times had Emily repeated those words to her? How many times had Bree repeated those words to students, clients, the loved ones of her patients? Those words had become a mantra for Bree, a sacred prayer etched lovingly along the borders of her energetic body, a guiding principle for her Work and her soul.

And now I know—it works both ways. She shivered. *Not only must I honor the choice of another's soul, I must uphold the choice of my own soul.*

"*For now that you have chosen,*" Bríde's voice rang through Bree, "*that choice holds you, now and for the rest of this lifetime.*"

Moaning softly, Bree exhaled. Her left hand slackened its grip and her *bodhrán* slid down over her knee to rest against the meditation cushion.

"It's official," Bree muttered. "Time to start anew."

Eyes closed, she lifted her head and straightened her spine. Her hair drifted across her cheeks and spilled down her back and shoulders. Sunlight shone warm and invitingly upon her face. Sweetness filled her mouth for a third time and she swallowed.

"Mother Bríghid, show me my way forward, back to living, back to Loving."

Bree opened her eyes. Golden sunlight flooded the room and cascaded around her. It enfolded her in a shimmering orb of radiance. The goddess' fiery eyes opened before her. Staring into them, Bree smiled.

"Blessed is the Mystery."

The soft chime of a Tibetan singing bowl seeped under the closed door. Bree swiveled toward the sound, then jerked back forward. Mother Bríghid was gone. Ordinary sunlight drifted through the window into the room.

Bree frowned.

Rising from her cushion, Bree returned her drum to its place beside the altar stone before opening the door. Her wool socks slipped on the oakwood floor as she crossed the hallway to the dining room table. Her telephone still rested beside her keys on the wooden surface. Picking it up, Fergus' face smiled at her. Bree clicked the message and read the text from her friend.

"Status change during the night. Please call to discuss."

34

As the soft chime of a Tibetan singing bowl spilled through the dining room, Bree's telephone vibrated in her hand. She dropped her gaze and flashing-blue eyes laughed at her from the picture on the screen. The words "*New text message: Tasha*" appeared before her.

Bree tilted her head. She tapped the new message icon and waited. She was not expecting a message from Tasha. *I hope everything is okay.*

"Hey! Eva's troupe is performing tomorrow night at Edison. Can I coax you out for the evening? How about I leave a ticket at Will Call?"

Bree tapped her finger on the side of the telephone. Bree and Gwen had been season ticket holders for the performing arts theatre on Washington University's main campus. But, like everything else, Bree had let their seats go when she left for Ireland. She really had not planned on needing them again.

"Could be fun," she postulated. A smile spreading across her face, she tapped out a response. "Sounds fabulous. Any chance of two tickets?"

Bree's telephone vibrated in her hand. A smiley face, its eyes bulging in surprise, lit up her screen and Bree chuckled.

"For you... sure!"

"Thanks," Bree typed her reply. "You are fabulous!"

Another smiley face grinned across her screen, this time blowing kisses. Bree pressed her fingers to her lips and blew a kiss back.

Closing out of her text messages, she pulled up Fergus' contact information, then pressed the green telephone icon. As she listened to the line ringing, she paced beside the dining room table.

A soft warmth slowly spilled down her left thigh. The line still ringing in her ear, Bree looked down. Crimson red blood seeped through her jeans' pocket.

Her feet slowed to a halt. She stood, hunched over and watched the blood ooze down the length of her pant leg. At the hem, the flow paused long enough to pool along the edge and send small droplets plunging to the floor. Before her eyes, blood soaked into her sock and pooled around her left foot.

"Hello, Bree?" Fergus' voice broke the silence.

Bree's head jerked up. She blinked her eyes, trying to wash the bloody spot out of her vision. "Hey, Fergus. I got your text message. What's up?"

"Pamela started bleeding again last night." Fergus sighed. "She said she had been feeling better since the journey, more like her old self. She even managed to cook herself dinner the past two nights. Then, out of the blue, it started again."

Bree closed her eyes. Quarreling voices drifted in from the Otherworld.

"She asked if you would be willing to meet her for another journey."

The sound of wood burning crackled around Bree. As reddish-orange firelight flickered through her inner vision, somewhere a woman wept.

"Tomorrow," Bree rubbed her eyes. "Tell her I will meet her again tomorrow. Just let me know what time works best for both of you."

"Thanks, Bree. I will be in touch as soon as I speak with her."

Bree opened her eyes. Lowering the telephone from her ear, she looked down at her feet. The blood was gone.

35

Midnight-black feathers dance and shiver on the wind as Bree sails upon silent wings. Beneath her, orange, red and gold leaves shimmer from horizon to horizon. Tree after tree of the ancient forest flames through her mind as Raven's searching eyes pierce the Otherworld.

"Pamela," Bree calls from her soul to her Allies. "I come in search of the healing that restores Pamela to wholeness."

Her wings pull taut. They tense and strain, banking against the heavy, moist, autumn currents. She arcs to the right, wings outstretched to hold the thermal. A break in the trees parts the forest below her and a deep, black circle seeps amidst the brilliant, flaming colors.

"Crrruck!"

Feathers slack and her wings drop. She leans into the wind, riding the currents in a great spiral downward, closer and closer to the earth. Crashing light, like lightning, sparks through Raven's eyes and glints across Bree's awareness. Blinded in the glare, her feet touch earth.

She is woman again. Her black hair drifting in the fading breeze, Bree rises from a crouch. Quarreling voices ricochet around her. Blinking hard to clear her vision, she lifts her head and opens her eyes.

The dais of the men's village stretches empty before her. To her right, the High King stands, hands on his hips, eyes glaring at the purple-robed priestess opposite him. The men of the village cluster together, encircling the two opponents in a living wall. As Bree scans the roiling scene, the crowd of men surges closer.

Silvery-blue light crackles down the arms of the priestess and churns in the palms of her hands. She stands, muscles tensed, green eyes glowering. "It is only fair."

"Fair?" The king steps closer to the woman. Barely controlled anger thrashes behind his words. "You dare speak to me of being fair?"

A deep, guttural sound like thunder rumbles through the amassed onlookers. The image of the Dagda—eyes narrowed and growling—flashes through Bree's awareness.

The priestess leans toward the man. Brilliant red flames burst from the ground beneath her. The flames lick up and around the sides of her energy body, encasing her in a blazing, neon sphere. Her eyes locked fiercely on her opponent, she stretches her hands wide and flicks her fingers. The flames around her sizzle as if doused with water, then disappear in small puffs of smoke.

She juts her chin. "You must do what is Right."

The High King slowly folds his arms across his chest. "Must?" His eyes rake the length of the auburn-haired woman. Lightning flashes between them as thunder rolls through the square. "You demand overmuch for someone so precariously situated."

Talons grip, stinging Bree's left shoulder, and she flinches. Turning her head sharply, Raven's feathers flap against her face. She closes her eyes and waits for her Ally to settle.

The priestess' voice rings through the square. "Return our Chalice!" The impassioned demand reverberates in Bree's ears. Crashing with the raging voice of the sea, it trembles down her limbs.

"I have told you already," the king's voice bites, "your Chalice is not here."

"Truth, Raven Child." Bree opens her eyes. Raven's dark gaze glistens before her. "Tell her, now."

Thunder rattles through the square. As the men press shoulder to shoulder around them, small flashes of searing light snap overhead. The caustic scent of ozone burns Bree's nose.

"He speaks the Truth."

Bree's voice flows into the scene. To her inner eye, the words pour a healing balm, shimmering in luminous, white light, like a river cascading between the two leaders. "Peace," Bree whispers mentally.

With a slow, deep breath, she calls to her Druid ancestors. "Great Peacemakers of old," she speaks from her soul, "if it is true, you could stop a war by walking between the armies, please, work that magic now."

The white waves of the river coalesce and deepen before her. Pink light splashes through the waters, etching each crest. As the waters rise, higher and higher, the waves spill outward and wash over both the High King and the Priestess before bathing the surrounding men. Spiraling in shimmering eddies, the pink waters recede into the earth and disappear.

"Love, Love, Love," Bree whispers into the growing silence.

The king unfolds his arms and stares at the waters sinking into the earth at his feet. His eyes scan up his still dry clothes. Shaking his head, mouth slightly agape, he raises curious eyes to Bree.

"Forgive me." Bree bows her head to the High King. "I meant no offense."

"Then none is taken," the soft voice of the priestess ripples through the square.

Bree bows her head in gratitude and greeting to the priestess, then returns her gaze to the High King.

He nods a slow greeting.

"Thank you." Bree presses her hand to her heart. "And thank you, Ancient Ones," her soul whispers to her Druid ancestors. Ghostly outlines flicker in her peripheral vision. One by one, the silhouettes flare, spiraling in incandescent blues, purples and greens to seal a circle of sheltering around them before fading from view.

Bree faces the priestess. "Sister," she takes a step closer to her, "He is correct. Your Chalice is not within this village."

The priestess shakes her head. "It must be here."

"No." Raven's voice clear within her, Bree steps closer still. "Only recently, you spoke these same words to him. Do you remember?"

A frown ripples across the priestess' brow. "Yes, but..."

"Your words were true, as true as his own are now."

Auburn hair spills down the sides of the woman's shaking head. Bree raises her arms to her sides. "Sister, please, look at me." Green eyes rise hesitantly and meet Bree's. "I can take you to your Chalice." Bree opens her palms to the woman and spreads her fingers wide. "Look. See the Truth of this for yourself."

Verdant green light flames around the woman, then rushes at Bree. As it meets Bree's energetic field, the flame splits into three and wraps around her. Weaving like a braid, the three flames race up her length. They spiral deiseal, sunwise, interlacing from her feet to her head. The three flames converge above her and a shower of brilliant, green sparks cascades around her to the ground. Bree watches the scintillating particles dowse themselves upon the earth of the square. When the last spark goes dark, the green flames around her suddenly disappear.

"Unchanged. The light remained green." The priestess sighs and raises questioning eyes to Bree. "How can this be?"

"Come." Bree extends her hand to the woman. "Let us show you."

36

"Crrruck!"

Midnight-black feathers flutter over Bree's head as she stands before a small, turf-covered, stone roundhouse. To her right, the priestess lifts curious, green eyes to track the grey smoke spiraling out of a gap under the roofing.

The priestess's eyes drift down the carefully crafted stone walls. "What is this place?"

"This," a woman's voice—ancient, yet youthful—ripples the chill, autumn air, "is the current resting place of your Spiral's Chalice."

Bree turns toward the familiar voice. The goddess Brighid stands in front of the roundhouse doorway. Golden-white light shimmers around her. It radiates outward and everything it touches vibrates with a deep, resonant hum.

Pressing her left hand to her heart, Bree bows her head in greeting. "Mother Brighid."

Purple blurs along the edges of her vision. Glancing out the corner of her eyes, Bree watches the priestess sink toward the earth in a deep curtsy. Auburn hair slips from the woman's shoulders as her head lowers in honoring and her hands fold over her heart.

"Blessed Mother." The priestess' voice is a whisper.

*Golden-white light washes over Bree and the priestess beside her.
"Síochán daoibh agus tá fáilte romhaibh," Bríghid's voice thrums through
her, "Peace and welcome, my daughters."*

*The deep humming flows the length of Bree and seeps into the ground
at her feet. Bree lifts her head and the priestess rises to standing.*

*"I don't understand." The priestess shakes her head. "Why would the
Chalice be here?"*

*Bríghid smiles, showering the woman in golden-white light once more.
She lifts her hand and offers it, palm open, to the priestess. "Come with me
and see."*

*The priestess places her hand onto Bríghid's open palm and the goddess
enfolds the long, delicate fingers in her own. Stepping to the side, Bríghid
pulls open the wooden door of the roundhouse. As she escorts the woman
into the stone structure, the goddess gestures for Bree to follow.*

*Bree steps into near darkness. Firelight flickers, the only light
illuminating the round room. To the left of the fireplace, a shadowy figure
hunches over a metal cauldron. Bree blinks her eyes. As she adjusts to the
low lighting, she recognizes the woman stirring the boiling liquid inside the
cauldron.*

"Deirdre." The priestess' voice bites coldly.

*The form stiffens beside the fire. Slowly, Deirdre removes the wooden
spoon from the mixture and places it on a stone beside the hearth. Wiping
her hands on her apron, she lifts her chin and glares at the priestess.*

*"I should have known." The priestess sighs. "What are you doing here?
And what have you done with the Chalice?"*

"What you would not."

The priestess furrows her brow. "Whatever do you mean?"

*Deirdre's eyes flash, shifting to gaze beyond the woman in front of her.
Bree turns to look over her right shoulder. There, half-hidden in the
flickering shadows, a woman lies listless upon a sheet stretched over a
mattress of birch leaves.*

*Bree takes a step toward the bed and stops. A dark stain seeps down the
side of the mattress.*

"Brónagh." The priestess crosses the small space to the bedside. Bending

over the woman, she rests her hand upon the woman's forehead as her eyes scan the wasting body.

Bree closes her eyes. "She is dying." *She opens her eyes and stares into the eyes of her Teacher.*

"Yes," *Brighid nods.* "Her life force, like her blood, spills slowly from her body."

"Why?" *Bree faces the goddess and takes a step closer to her.* "What is the source of this wounding, and what may be done to heal it for the highest good of all?"

Brighid lifts her gaze to glare at Deirdre. "A Hallow wrongly taken always yields Unraveling. Only Right Relationship may birth Balance and Healing. Anything else leads to illness and death."

Bree glances from Brighid to Deirdre and back again. As woman and goddess stare at each other in rigid silence, Bree shakes her head. "I don't understand."

The priestess rises from the bed and walks toward the hearth. "Child..." *Her voice is tender, softened with sorrow.* "What have you done?"

Deirdre stares at the priestess. Through the silence, the fire snaps and hisses through the roundhouse.

"Brónagh wanted a child." *Brighid's voice flows, radiating warmth.* "Do you remember, Sister? She came to you, begged you to help her conceive."

"Yes," *the priestess nods.* "But I could not help her. I tried many remedies, each without result."

"But Deirdre believed she knew better." *Edged with censure, Brighid's voice stings and Bree winces.* "She had advanced far enough in the Spiral's healing arts—under your good tutelage, Sister—to learn of the Chalice. She believed Its Power would quicken her sister's belly. So, she took It from Its place of honoring and brought It to her sister."

Bree shifts toward Deirdre and looks her full in the face. "She took It without permission, usurped Its Power without the right to do so."

"And the Power turned to Unraveling." *The priestess looks from sister to sister.* "Instead of offering healing, It claimed her sister's life force and now slowly siphons it away."

Bree turns to face her Teacher. "And the Blade?"

Bríghid raises blazing eyes to Deirdre. The novice flinches and looks away.

The goddess sighs. "When she failed using the Chalice alone, she searched for another solution. She remembered the Great Loving, the ritual of bringing Chalice and Blade together in Sacred Creation. Although unschooled in Its Mysteries, she decided to invoke the ritual and stole the Blade in preparation."

"Great Mother, no." *Horror pales the priestess' green eyes and she swings around to face her novice.* "Oh child... you didn't..."

Sorrow moans through Bree. Swallowing hard, she shakes her head. "No. She didn't. Fortunately, she was spotted and pursued. In the resulting chaos, she must have prayed for help and found me." *She looks at the woman trembling beside the fire. Tears pool in Bree's eyes.* "You realize, you would have killed your sister... instantly."

Deirdre's eyes widen. She inhales slowly and her trembling disappears behind an overlay of rigidity. "How do you know?"

"Because every act of Creation requires sufficient energy to engender Manifestation." *The priestess looks back at Brónagh unconscious in the bed.* "Your intention required life force to come into reality and your ritual drew that life force from your sister." *She looks back at Deirdre.* "Had you trusted in the Goddess, not presumed beyond your training, you could have avoided this sorrow, Deirdre. Yours and hers."

The dark stain seeps wider and spills down the side of the mattress. Before Bree's eyes, blood pools on the earthen floor. She draws a slow breath. "Where is the Chalice now?"

Silence stretches around Bree. She turns toward the hearth. The fire still burns behind Deirdre but Bree cannot hear its crackling. She studies the woman and realizes Deirdre's lips are moving but no sound escapes from them. Peering more deeply, Bree sees a series of runes shimmering across the woman's energy field.

"A spell of silence." *The priestess scowls.* "I taught you better than this, Deirdre." *She presses her hands to her hips, but the woman by the fire does not move.* "Very well, I will find it myself."

"Wait." *Bríghid's warmth breathes through the small room. The goddess crosses to stand in front of Deirdre.* "I know you love your sister. I *know, too—in your own way—you acted out of Love. So I offer Love back to you now. If your sister is to recover, and you are ever to progress, you must undo the damage you have done."*

Deirdre lifts pleading eyes to the goddess.

Bríghid shakes her head. "You, yourself, and no other."

Silvery light flashes and the snapping crackle of the fire fills Bree's ears. Startled, she closes her eyes at the sudden rush of sound and steadies herself. When she opens them again, Deirdre hunches over her sister's bed.

The novice's hand disappears into the mattress of birch leaves and re-emerges, clasping the Chalice. Silvery-white, the ceramic vessel gleams from an inner radiance all Its own. The light streams outward from Its edges and the room around Bree brightens.

Deirdre hesitates. Her eyes gaze longingly at the ceramic vessel shimmering in her hand. In the bed beside her, Brónagh stirs. Deirdre drops her gaze to the shifting form and waits. When her sister remains unconscious in the bed, Deirdre faces Bríghid.

"Very well. What must I do?"

"The Chalice must be re-consecrated—cleansed and blessed anew in the Sacred Fire of the Goddess—and returned to Its rightful place of Honoring."

Deirdre stares at the goddess. Frowning, she takes a step toward the door. Bríghid's voice stops her short.

"And... you must apologize."

37

Golden-white light flashes, like sunlight dancing upon water, and Bree closes her eyes. The chilly, earthen floor of the roundhouse falls away, and a gentle warmth presses firmly against her bare feet. A deep, droning tone breaks the shimmering silence. Reverberating beneath her, it rises from the earth, surges up her legs and pools in her pelvis. Inhaling the flowing power, Bree opens her eyes.

Flames stretch and flicker before her. Crimson-orange, they cast their heat from the sunken, clay brazier that holds them. Their warmth flows across the stones pressed into the earthen floor and seeps into Bree's feet.

Images coil and spiral beyond the corners of Bree's eyes. She turns her head and lets her gaze drift along the earthen walls encircling her. In the flickering light, dark shapes and lines undulate across the concave surfaces. Then they roil toward her, reaching for her arms, her hair, her legs. Bree holds her breath. The deep droning surges out her pelvis and floods up her spine to her neck, before pouring down her shoulders and out her hands. Surprised by the sudden rush of power, Bree inhales sharply.

She blinks, and the coiling tendrils are gone. Returned to their earthen walls, they stretch and spiral in the flickering light of the fire as the deep, droning tone recedes into the ground around her.

A soft, hollow tinkling fills her ears. Too deep to be a chime, it whispers above the crackling of the flames. Bree turns back toward the fire, burning at the center of the cave. Through the flames she sees them.

Two women uncurl folded legs and rise slowly from the cavern floor on the other side of the fire. The dark spirals and lines painted on their skin undulate as they move. To Bree's eyes, the markings snake down their bodies, wrapping them in living, writhing power. Small bones dangle from headbands woven of black, red and white thread. Clinking together, the bones whisper their eerie blessing to the gathering.

Voices drift just beyond her hearing and Bree shivers. "The voices of the dead," she murmurs.

"The voice of Rebirth," Bríghid whispers in her ear.

Bree looks to her left, into the eyes of her Teacher. "What is this place?"

The goddess smiles, golden-white light shimmering and enfolding her like a halo in the half-light of the cave. Then she shifts her gaze and nods to the priestess. "Sister, if you please."

With quiet acceptance, the auburn-haired woman bows her head to the goddess. Rising slowly, the priestess steps toward the fire. She bows again, this time to the two women beyond the flames. The soft, hollow tinkling rustles their reply.

The three women stare into the fire. As the small bones chatter, the priestess lifts her hand and gestures. "Come, Deirdre."

Feet shuffle upon stone behind Bree, and she pivots. Deirdre stands in the shadows. Despite the summons, the novice backs slowly away from the gathering.

Gazing intently into the flames, the priestess frowns. "Come."

Bríghid turns narrowed eyes upon the novice and Bree shudders. Deirdre's eyes lock with those of the goddess and she halts mid-step. Planting her feet wide, Deirdre balls her right hand into a fist. Power, like heat lightning, snaps and sizzles along her arm.

"Deirdre," Bree urges, "stop this. You will not win." Before her eyes, the novice slowly raises her fist. Bree starts to step toward the woman, then forces herself back. The choice, she knows, is not hers to make.

Heat sears past her, blazing out from Deirdre's opening hand and lashing toward the goddess.

Bree gasps. "No!"

Eyes locked on the brazen woman, Brighid parts her lips and blows. One short, soft puff, and no more. The wall of heat bounces off the goddess's breath. Recoiling in upon itself, it thrashes and whirls wildly as it hurtles back toward the novice.

The roiling ball of heat implodes. Flames leap and blaze. They lash in all directions and arc just clear of Deirdre's face.

The last flame sputters and shatters into embers. Cascading slowly, one by one they hit the stone floor of the cavern and extinguish themselves.

Deirdre stares from the shadows.

Brighid raises her eyebrows. "Well?"

"Please, Deirdre. You have come this far." Bree steps forward. "Remember, yours is not the only life at stake here. What you choose now will mean life or death for your sister, too."

"And the others."

Bree's head whirls toward her Teacher. "Others?"

The goddess nods. "Her sisters of the Spiral. Their lives, too, will be impacted. She can choose life for them all, or death and hardship."

Fire blazes through Bree, blurring her vision. Within the crimson-orange flames, an image of Deirdre's sister, Brónagh, rises before Bree. Silvery-blue light seeps from the mattress of birch leaves beneath the dying woman. The translucent rays race through the Otherworld, seeking the energy needed to maintain the Working. One after another, unknown women stumble and fall before Bree. Blood streams down their bodies and pools upon green earth.

"Pamela," Bree chokes.

With a golden flash, Bree's vision clears and she takes another step toward Deirdre. Blinking back tears, she shakes. "How many would you sacrifice? How many would you condemn?"

Deirdre lifts her chin. Crossing her arms over her chest, she tucks the Spiral's Chalice carefully into the crook of her elbow.

Bree's shoulders droop. "How will you explain it to them, the ones you called sister? The ones who cultivated life here in this Spiral with you? How will you explain your choice to them?"

Shadowy figures emerge out of the darkness of the cavern. One by one, they shudder, light coalescing into form, and walk toward the woman. *Their mouths slowly opening, they call the novice's name.* "Deirdre..."

The ghostly women press closer to Deirdre, encircling her. A dark-haired woman pushes to the front and extends reaching arms toward the novice. Deirdre stifles a sob.

"Keep going," *Brighid's voice echoes within Bree.* "Speak what must be said."

"What will you tell my client, Pamela? How will you explain to Brónagh that you usurped her right to choose for herself?"

Deirdre's eyes widen and meet Bree's. Hugging the Chalice to her chest, Deirdre mutters. "Choice is a sacred right."

Bree nods. "And a soul's choice must be honored."

Pale bluish light shivers on the air before Bree. As it stretches into the translucent form of a woman, Bree hears Deirdre's breath catch.

"Brónagh."

"Sister." *The dark-haired woman glides toward Deirdre, her soul light sputtering fiercely. To Bree's eyes, the woman's soul force wanes dangerously thin.* "Please, sister." *The ghostly woman hovers just in front of Deirdre.* "Give me back my right to choose."

Deirdre's body shakes. With a deep, guttural moan, the novice's shoulders shudder. Tears spill from her eyes as, sobbing, she drops her head. "Sister... I'm sorry." *Deirdre lifts her head.* "I am so sorry."

Brónagh's ghostly form steps close enough to enfold Deirdre in ethereal arms. "If that is so, will you do something for me?"

Deirdre lifts her tear-streaked face.

"Will you restore the Chalice to Its rightful place?"

Deirdre drops her gaze to the Chalice.

"Please," *Brónagh lifts her sister's chin with flickering fingers.* "Honor my right to choose and set us all free."

38

Bree shifted her legs and reversed their fold underneath her on the purple meditation cushion. The sage-green walls of Fergus' treatment room stretching around her, she stared into the flickering candle on the altar. For a moment, she could almost see Brónagh's wraithlike fingers withdrawing into the flame.

She sighed. Blinking back tears, she looked up at the two sisters seated on the other side of the altar. *So much sorrow.* Both women watched her, their eyes slightly widened and fixed on her. *Great Mother, let the sorrow end here.*

Pamela leaned forward. "Bree, please... Did Deirdre surrender the Chalice?"

Bree scanned the woman's face. Too little flesh still hung from the protruding cheekbones, but blue fire again flashed within the sapphire eyes. *Give her time.*

Slowly, Bree nodded. "They did it together."

Pamela sat back and exhaled.

"With Brónagh at her side, Deirdre returned the Chalice to the fire at the heart of the cave. The Priestess and the two Keepers of the Sacred Flame then completed the ritual of Hallowing to reconsecrate the Chalice. As the Chalice emerged renewed from the flames, Deirdre fell to her knees and cried."

Bree's eyes sought those of Pamela. "Brónagh held her sister until she could cry no more. Then, I heard her whisper into Deirdre's ear —'Sister, I forgive you.' Her voice sounded very much like yours."

Pamela started. "Mine?"

Tears pooled in Bree's eyes. She blinked them away and nodded. "The two sisters watched as the Priestess restored the Chalice to Its altar. Neither were allowed to touch It or come near It after the re-Hallowing." She shrugged. "Neither were initiated to a level that entitled them to such contact. So the Priestess returned It to Its rightful place on their behalf."

Bree stared into the candle flame, burning on the altar. Silvery-blue eyes blinked from the Otherworld. *"Finish it. Tell them,"* Brónagh's voice urged.

"Is it over?"

Blue eyes gleamed in the half-light as Pamela stared at Bree.

"It is," Bree sighed. "But, at a cost. Deirdre can no longer abide in the women's Spiral." Her eyes flowed from sister to sister. "Deirdre chose to come into active, conscious relationship with the Blade. In fact, she physically *placed* herself in relationship with It. She came just short of invoking Its Power. That action and *interaction* has caused her *Orán Croí*, the song of her soul, to change."

"Which means?" Kat's voice cracked.

"The purpose of her soul is forever changed. She can no longer remain with those who cultivate the pure energy of the Chalice. Since she has chosen to be in relationship with the Blade, she must live with those who cultivate Its energy. She must move to a new soul village, a new soul family, one whose members have been touched by the Chalice but live by the Blade."

Bree let her gaze drift back to the candle. "My Teacher has escorted her there. Alone."

"What about Brónagh?"

Bree faced Pamela. *She understands.* "Brónagh made no such choice. She has returned to the Soul Spiral with the Priestess."

Pamela closed her eyes. "Without her sister." Her left hand reached to her side in search of Kat's. After the third attempt, Pamela glanced at her sister. The fair-haired head hung low over the woman's chest and her folded hands disappeared into her lap.

Bree paused. Emotion, raw and unnamable, seeped from Kat's slumped form.

"It's me." Kat's shoulders shook. She lifted her head and tears slipped down her cheeks. "I was Deirdre. I *am* Deirdre." She dropped her head in her hands. "Sister, I am sorry. I am so sorry."

39

Kat lifted her head. Tears spilled slowly down her cheeks as she stared silently into the past. Bree watched the churning soul light swirl around the woman. Brilliant oranges, purples and reds roiling through her inner vision, she waited. *Love, Love, Love*, her soul whispered.

"I am the older sister." Kat's voice ached, rough and strained. Her eyes met Bree's. "I raised Pamela after our mother died. Did you know that?"

Bree shook her head.

"At first, I hated her for it." Kat dropped her gaze to her hands. "I was ten years old when mother died. One day, I was a child, carefree and playing with my friends. The next, I was a mother, with a scared six-year-old in my care." Kat's hands clenched in her lap. "I can still hear our father's voice. The night of mother's funeral, he sat me down. He looked so old. I remember wondering how long it would be before he left us, too. He sat there a long time, just staring at his hands. Then he looked at me and said, 'You are the only mother she has now. Remember that, always.' We never spoke of it again. But, after that, he just left her in my care. And my childhood died."

Kat raised her head. Bree shifted to meet the woman's gaze, but Kat's eyes stared through her, still searching the past.

"Later, I came to love Pamela. Truly. I even began to think of her as my own child. But the damage was already done. You see, I was so angry with her for stealing my youth. For years, I laid awake at night wishing Pamela would know what it was like to be denied something she desperately wanted, to be denied the joy of childhood." The fair-haired woman closed her eyes and shuddered.

Kat turned and met her sister's gaze. "I knew it was my fault, you see. My childish anger had interfered." Tears slid down her cheeks. "I took away your right to choose." Kat's voice broke. Her shoulders shaking, she sobbed silently.

"That's why you offered to carry a child for me when I couldn't." Pamela's voice flowed soft through the half-lit circle. She shifted to her knees and reached for her sister, but Kat pushed her arms away.

"You don't understand..." Kat shook her head. "You wanted a child so badly. What was it you said?"

Resting her hands on her thighs, Pamela settled onto her knees. "I wanted the chance to create something beautiful and loving."

"And I so wanted you to have that chance. I wanted to give that back to you. But every time we tried to conceive, I just got angry and you would bleed again."

"Yes." Pamela nodded. "That's when I started hemorrhaging. But, sister," she leaned forward to look into Kat's eyes, "that wasn't your fault."

"Yes, it was. Each time we waited to see if I was pregnant, I just kept thinking—she is doing it again. She is forcing motherhood upon me. And I would lie awake at night, torn between my childish anger and the love I feel for you now." Kat blinked, loosing fresh tears. "I wanted this for you so badly. I even went for acupuncture to make it happen. But my old anger just got in the way." The fair-haired woman shook.

Bree nodded. "And each time the two of you tried to conceive," her voice flowed gently, the golden-white light of Bríghid shimmering with each word from the flame into the circle, "you activated

Deirdre's magic. Then the Chalice claimed the required life force for the Working, and Brónagh and Pamela bled."

Pamela stared at Bree. Blue fire flashed deep within the woman's sapphire eyes and Bree sighed. *So much sorrow. Great Mother, let it end here.*

Golden-white light pooled around the two sisters. Before Bree's eyes, two Otherworldly arms stretched across their shoulders as the goddess Bríghid shimmered between them. Smiling softly, the goddess kissed first Kat's forehead, then Pamela's.

"Sister." Kat's voice trembled. "I am sorry. I am so sorry."

Pamela dropped her gaze to the floor.

A heartbeat pounded in Bree's ears. The throbbing rhythm stretched and deepened until the deep, droning tone of her journey ached through her body. As Bríghid's hands slid down the two women's backs and rested behind their hearts, Bree pressed her palms upon the floor and the throbbing tone pulsed into the circle.

Silvery-purple light seeped outward from Bree. Wave upon wave, the light rolled. Like an Otherworldly surf, it washed across the circle and bathed the two sisters.

Bree's eyes met Bríghid's. *Love, Love, Love.*

Pamela rose onto her knees and wrapped her arms around her sobbing sister. Hugging Kat tightly, Pamela kissed the fair hair and whispered, "I forgive you."

40

The two dancers wound their way across the stage of Washington University's Edison Theatre. From her seat tucked off the left-center aisle, Bree watched the lithe bodies stretch, arc and whirl in a continuous sequence of graceful, fluid movements.

As the man and woman flowed together, ebbed apart and spiraled back together, again and again, Bree's mouth slowly fell open. She could see the Truth at the heart of their performance, as if painted in the air before her. The pulsing pattern of the dance linked them, intertwined them in unspeakable intimacy.

Her breath caught. *The Chalice and the Blade.*

Bree glanced to her right and peeked at Hamish in the seat beside her. *Does he see it, too? Or is it just a dance to him?*

His eyes shifted to hers. Heat shivered under her skin and her cheeks burned. She knew they were slowly turning red, but she would not look away.

The haunting music waned and, in its place, a heartbeat pulsed through the silent theatre. As the deep, throbbing echo faded, the audience around Bree erupted in applause. With a soft smile, Hamish blinked, breaking the connection holding her. Bree exhaled and, looking back at the bowing dancers, added her own applause to the room.

Hamish leaned toward her. His breath soft on her neck, he spoke into her ear. "So, tha's Tasha's lass?"

Bree nodded. "Eva. Beautiful, isn't she?"

Hamish angled his head to catch a glimpse of the dancers rising from another bow. Bree watched his eyes scan the length of the woman's lean torso.

"I can see where ye might say tha'. But, she's no my cup a tea."

The stage again empty, light slowly filled the theatre and the people around her began rising from their seats. Bree slid forward in her seat and looked back at him. "No?"

Dark eyes twinkling, Hamish stood and offered Bree his hand. A soft grin curling the edges of her mouth, she placed her hand in his and rose to her feet. His fingers closed around hers and he drew her toward him until her hand rested upon his chest.

"No."

"Excuse me." A woman with crisp, blonde hair leaned around Hamish. "Do you mind?"

Bree followed the woman's gesture to the empty space behind her. *Someone's in a hurry.* She smiled at the woman. "Sorry." Turning to make her way out of the row of seats, she let her hand slide from Hamish's chest. But he did not let go.

As the line of people filing toward the aisle slowed, Bree glanced back at their joined hands.

Am I sure about this?

She inched with the crowd up the aisle steps and spotted a familiar face. Braids loose and flowing down bare shoulders, Tasha stood in the open space at the top of the theatre's left bank of seats. Bree smiled. Tightening her grip on Hamish's hand, she guided him through the milling people toward her friend.

Tasha pressed cheek to cheek with a tall woman whose cropped, red hair blazed above an olive green, fitted evening suit. After offering Tasha a parting word, the woman turned and headed toward the exit. Bree cleared the top step just as Tasha turned.

A smile raced across Tasha's heart-shaped face. "Bree!"

Bree beamed. "I was hoping to catch you."

The man standing to her left headed toward the exit and Bree moved into the opening. As she did, Hamish stepped forward to stand beside her. The deep blue of his fine MacLeod hunting tartan shimmied just above his muscular knees.

Gleaming, grey-blue eyes darted from Bree's face to Hamish's and back again, before tracking down her arm to her hand, still folded in his. Lifting her gaze to Bree's, Tasha's eyes rounded in surprise.

Bree's cheeks blazed. Clearing her throat, she withdrew her hand from Hamish's and instantly regretted it. "Tasha, this is a friend of mine, Hamish MacSween. He's visiting from Scotland." Grateful for a reason to escape her friend's questioning gaze, she almost sighed. "Hamish, I'd like you to meet Tasha Ellis. Tasha helps with the business side of the café."

Bowing his head, Hamish reached out and shook hands with Tasha. "*Is deas bualadh leat...*" his deep burr rumbled, "tis lovely to meet ye."

Tasha grinned. "Likewise."

Hamish tilted his head to face Bree. "Gwen's café?"

"That's right." Bree nodded, her cheeks flaming anew. "And she was kind enough to get us tickets for tonight's performance."

"Och, aye?" He turned back to Tasha. "Twas kind of ye, lass." His brow furrowed. "I remember now. Bree mentioned ye. She said Eva, that lovely dancer, is your partner."

"It's true," Tasha chuckled. "She is."

Bree's shoulders lurched as someone bumped into her from behind. She turned sideways in an effort to allow the person to pass and stared into familiar green eyes.

"Pardon me. I'm so sor..." Chelle stammered, then fell silent.

Bree shook her head slowly. As she struggled through her surprise for words of greeting, a striking woman in a flowing, silvery-grey dress crested the steps and wrapped an alabaster-skinned arm around Chelle's waist. She leaned close, spilling long, dark hair down milky, bare shoulders, and murmured in Chelle's ear. "*Vseo khorosho?*"

Blushing slightly, Chelle faced the woman and nodded. With a sultry smile, the woman's azure eyes slid with her free hand up Chelle's arm to rest on her neck. "*Poideomte.*" She tilted her head toward the exit as her hand drifted down Chelle's back. "Let's go."

In stunned silence, Bree watched the two women walk away hand in hand. A few paces before the doors, Chelle turned to face Bree. Her cheeks blazing red, she mouthed, "Sorry." Then she disappeared into the night.

Tasha's voice drifted through the emptying theatre. "Is this your first time in St. Louis?"

"Aye."

"How long are you staying?"

Bree's eyebrows arched and fell. With a quick shake of her head, she shifted her position and rejoined the conversation. Hamish's brown eyes studied her. "I cannae say."

"Tasha." A man in faded jeans appeared beside Bree's friend. Tied into a fierce top knot, his silvering hair pulled tight against his head. "Ready?"

"Sure, Grey." Tasha smiled before turning back to Bree. "I have to go. Grey is my escort backstage. Can you come to the café tomorrow? I have a few things I'd like to discuss."

"Of course." Bree leaned forward and hugged Tasha. "Any particular time?"

"No. I'll be there all day, so whatever time works best for you." Tasha stepped back and smiled at Hamish. "I hope to see you again before you leave. But, if not, enjoy your stay." She cocked an eyebrow. "I'm sure Bree will take excellent care of you."

41

Bree stepped out of Mallinckrodt Center and stood looking up into the evening sky. *Quite the night.*

She dropped her gaze and looked back at the building. Letting the glass door fall closed behind him, Hamish strode toward her. As his kilt billowed slightly in the cool breeze, a smile spread across her face. *And it isn't over yet.*

"Are ye cold?"

"No," Bree shook her head. "Would you mind walking a bit? I don't have many reasons to come to campus anymore. Might be nice to see it," she tilted her head, "to share it with you."

"Aye," a slow grin tugged the corners of Hamish's mouth. "A wee wander would be just the thing."

Bree followed the paved-stone sidewalk toward the Danforth University Center. Affectionately called the DUC, the ultra-modern and LEED-NC Gold social center replaced Mallinckrodt as the campus's primary meeting, eating and general gathering space almost as soon as it opened. As pleased as she was to see her alma mater investing in green construction standards, Bree mourned the loss of the simple comforts, like Holmes Lounge and the green chairs that, in her day, populated Mallinckrodt's lower level.

Everything changes. The fire of Creation ever burns.

She sighed.

Hamish glanced at her from the corner of his eyes. "Are ye all right?"

Bree nodded and gestured to her right. "Come this way."

Leaving the DUC to the current generation's night-owls, she strolled along the curving, crushed-stone walkway past Umrath Hall toward one of the remaining open green spaces on the Hilltop Campus. The toes of her boots just touching the grass, she stared across the lawn, past the raised, rod-iron fence, to McMillan Hall.

Silvery light glinted above the grassy plaza at the heart of the u-shaped building. Pooling slowly, it spilled ghostly images before Bree's eyes. A rectangular, woven picnic basket sat with its lid flung open upon a well-worn, tan-colored stadium blanket. As a translucent hand reached into the basket, Bree shivered.

She blinked—once, twice—but the shimmering scene remained. Then, Gwen turned her ghostly face to Bree and laughed.

Bree closed her eyes and folded her arms around herself. Gwen had surprised her that day, brought her lunch and a moment of respite amidst an endless, exhausting Thursday.

Warmth spread across her back and wrapped over her shoulders. She opened her eyes. Gwen's silvery form, along with her lover's favorite blanket and basket, were gone. Hamish stood beside her, pulling his jacket more snuggly around her shoulders.

"I saw—ye were shivering."

"*Tapadh leat...*" Bree blinked back tears. "Thanks, Hamish."

His dark curls danced in the breeze. They were so close, her cheek tingled from their soft caress. He tugged his jacket tightly around her. "Better?"

"Mmmm-hmmm."

He looked up at her. "So, this is your school?"

"It used to be."

"Do ye no feel a part of it still?"

Bree shrugged. "It's changed a lot since I was here. Sometimes I hardly recognize it."

The deep tolling of a church bell rang into the night and Bree turned to her right. The twin spires of Graham Chapel stretched up to the purpling sky. Bree let her eyes drift along the pale stone of the front wall and down the three tiers of arching, stained-glass windows depicting the dedication of King Solomon's temple.

"*Tha e gu bòidheach...*" Hamish's deep burr rumbled beside her.

She turned to face him. "Yes," she whispered. "It is beautiful. It is my favorite building here."

The church bell continued tolling the hour for the campus community to hear and Bree counted silently. *Nine... ten... eleven.*

Hamish's deep brown eyes watched her.

I could kiss him. Right here. Now. Her heart pounded. *Then I would know.*

She stepped closer.

Silvery light glinted just beyond Hamish's shoulder. Bree shifted her gaze to the lawn stretching behind him and Gwen's ghostly form smiled.

Bree's breath caught. Dropping her head, she took a step away from him. "It's late. I should get you back to the hotel."

"Mmmmmmmmph."

White cotton shirt glinting in the moonlight, Hamish lifted his elbow and silently offered her his arm.

Heat flashed along her cheekbones, but, grasping the front of his jacket with one hand, she wrapped her other arm around his. She steered him back toward Umrath Hall.

"I, ahh... thought I'd visit the Arch tomorrow." Hamish peered at her. "Would ye join me?"

Bree dipped her chin to hide a grimace. "I can't. I have to meet Tasha at the café and run a few errands. But," she looked up at him, "you should go."

"I could wait, go another time. Together."

"It's not really my cup of tea. Besides," she smiled, "I've been too many times already."

"Well," his eyes found hers, "if you're certain."

Bree nodded and leaned closer to him.

They strolled on in silence. As they passed Umrath Hall, she glanced over her shoulder. Gwen's silvery form stood on the lawn, watching them leave.

42

Bree crossed the front patio, weaving her way between the crowded tables toward the front door. Her eyes flowed along the curling symbol of the fleur-de-lys printed across its glass surface to the words Café de Lys.

A few feet before the door, she stopped and stared at the familiar, white logo. She waited. When no blood spilled from the image, she exhaled and pulled open the door.

Sunlight streamed through the floor-to-ceiling windows. Like the tables outside, the overstuffed sofas teemed with guests enjoying coffee made their way and drinking in the golden radiance. Even Bree's favorite loveseat was already occupied.

Thank you, Great Mother. Bree bowed her head. *Blessed is Your bounty.*

The distinct hiss of the milk steamer whirred to life. Walking through the open room, Bree spotted Sheila's curly, red hair peeking out above the rumbling espresso machine. Two customers waited at the counter as Sheila worked her own, unique magic with the metal frothing pitcher.

Bree crossed the last few feet to the wooden door marked "Employees Only." She leaned her back against the wood and grasped the metal knob. Sheila's eyes suddenly shifted and met Bree's.

After a quick smile, Bree mouthed, "Need anything?"

Sheila tossed her head, sending rosy curls tumbling in all directions. With a wink, she looked back down at the frothing milk.

A woman in her element. Chuckling softly, Bree stepped into the back hallway and let the door fall closed behind her.

"No, no. no," Tasha's clipped voice spilled from the back office. "That's *not* what we agreed. I have the contract right here in my hands. If you need refreshing, I can send you a copy. Will email suffice? I am sure I have a copy in PDF."

Bree shortened her stride until she stood waiting in the half-lit corridor. Within the silence, the chaffing grate of a sharpening stone on metal rasped through her awareness.

"Ahhh, so you *do* remember the *actual* terms. Excellent." Tasha paused. "Mmmmm-hmmm. I am sure you are. Still, it would be best if I never had to have this conversation with you again. Agreed?"

A broad grin flooded Bree's face. She had been wise to offer the office manager position to Tasha. Now more than ever, she knew no one could handle it better.

"Well, now that you ask. A discount on our next delivery might make a lovely, heartfelt apology. Shall we say fifty percent?"

Bree's eyebrows arched upward. *Strong, wise and bold. Fabulous woman.*

"That is so very thoughtful," Tasha all but purred while still, somehow, sounding quite infuriated. "Yes, yes. You, too."

A soft thud spilled from the office and Bree wondered if she would need to replace Tasha's telephone.

She took a step forward, then halted. *A little warning might be better.* "Tasha?" Her voice echoed around her. "Are you back there?"

"Bree?" Footsteps rapped against the wooden floorboards. Then Tasha's heart-shaped face popped around the office door. She frowned. "What are you doing standing in the hallway?"

"I didn't want to intrude."

"Don't be silly." Tasha pushed the door all the way open and gestured to Bree. "Come in."

Bree stepped through the doorway and stifled a gasp. Tasha had redecorated.

Plain, black, plastic banker's boxes now tidily hugged the wall where Gwen's array of orange, red and purple storage containers once sprawled in apparent disorder. Bree had never managed to decipher Gwen's filing system. But Tasha's boxes each displayed a clear and neatly printed label. The colorful posters of all the places Gwen figured she would never see in person were stripped from the room, leaving the plain, simple, pinkish stone walls completely bare.

Just breathe.

Bree forced herself to exhale.

"You okay, Bree?"

Struggling to convince her rigid body to relax, Bree pivoted toward Tasha's voice. As her gaze fell upon the broad, wooden desk, she choked back a sob.

Tasha was beside her in an instant. Strong arms supporting her, Bree fought her way back to calm.

"I'm sorry." Tasha's voice soothed a tender balm upon Bree. "I forgot. You haven't been here since..."

"No." Bree's voice rasped in her throat. She wanted to say more, but the words just would not come.

She is really gone.

Bree leaned against the pristine desktop. "I've never seen it so clean." Her voice cracked.

Tasha's hand rested on Bree's back, steadying her. "I'm sorry. I shouldn't have redone everything."

"Of course you should have." Blinking back tears, Bree turned her head to face Tasha. "It looks lovely. Truly."

Tasha's eyebrows arched in silent inquiry.

"I mean it. Much more my style." Bree chuckled, despite herself. "I never could stomach Gwen's raucous taste in décor."

She ran her hands slowly across the clean, wooden surface. "I'd almost forgotten what the top looked like. How beautifully the grain spirals through the wood." A tear broke free and spilled down her cheek and onto the polished surface. "It must have taken you a day just to clear it."

"A week, actually." Tasha's sigh washed over Bree's aching soul. "How Gwen knew where everything was is a mystery to me. But, I gotta hand it to her. She did. When I finally managed to sort through it all, everything was precisely up to date."

Bree pushed herself upright. "Still," she gestured to the black, plastic boxes, "I think this will be much more efficient."

Tasha leaned forward and stared into Bree's eyes.

"It was just a shock." Bree grimaced. "I'm okay. Really."

"I'll just ask Sheila to make you an Americano..."

Tasha was already back on the other side of the desk, her telephone in her hand, before Bree could object. "No, please. Don't bother her. She has enough to do with that packed house."

"You're sure?"

Bree nodded.

Tasha's flashing, grey-blue eyes scanned Bree head to toe and back again. "All right," she lowered the telephone to the desk. "But, if you change your mind..."

"I promise," Bree smiled, "I will ask."

"Why don't we sit?" Tasha stepped out from behind the desk and gestured to the back corner of the office. "We can talk more comfortably over there."

Letting her fingertips drift along the wooden desktop, Bree worked her way around the central piece of furniture. As she did, a small, round black-metal café table and two matching chairs came into view.

"Thanks again for the tickets to last night's performance." Bree settled into the open chair, placing her back deliberately to the desk. "Eva was magnificent. That last piece left me breathless."

"It's called *Creation*." Tasha's hands pressed to her heart. "So beautiful. Eva and Dean worked on it endlessly. She will be so pleased it touched you." A grin spread slowly across her face. "And Hamish, did he enjoy it?"

Heat flamed, staining Bree's cheeks red. "He did."

"Lovely legs."

"It's not what you think."

"Bree," Tasha leaned forward and rested an elbow on the small table, "the man is clearly in love with you. I think 'besotted' is the word. The question is—are you ready to acknowledge your own feelings for him?"

Bree opened her mouth to object. "I... it isn't quite..." she stammered, then slumped forward in silence. She buried her face in her hands. "Go ahead, say it."

"Say what?"

"That I've lost my mind. That I'm a traitor. That you will no longer speak to me if I decide to date him."

"Why would I do that?" Tasha reached out and pulled Bree's hands away from her face. "I've had my own share of male lovers."

Bree sat back in the chair. "You mean..."

"Yes," Tasha smiled. "I'm bi." She shrugged. "Eva and I have been together for years. But, before her, my previous two lovers were men."

"I never knew."

"I rather prefer to keep my private life...well, private."

Bree stared at the woman she thought she knew well. For a moment, she wondered if she should be relieved or terribly concerned that she did not.

She searched Tasha's face. "Why tell me now?"

"Because," Tasha sighed, "I know just how difficult it is— acknowledging the feelings as real, trying to fight them or wishing them away, then making the decision to explore what others will condemn you for doing. You're right to brace yourself for the worst. You will likely lose a few friends over the choice." She reached across the table and rested her hand on top of Bree's. "But not me."

"Thanks," Bree placed her hand on top of Tasha's. "I really needed to hear that."

Tasha squeezed Bree's hands then sat back in her chair. "Here's my advice. Whatever you decide, whatever happens, remember this

—it's not about biology or anatomy. It's not even a matter of cultural norms. It's about Love. Or, at least, it should be."

The steady, soaking patter of pacific-northwest rain echoed out of Bree's memory. In her inner vision, Bree was back in Seattle. She stood with her aunt in her cousine Rose's guest bedroom. Emily's eyes danced between the rain beyond the bedroom window and Bree.

Bree closed her eyes. The rain slowly melting back into the Otherworld, she muttered Emily's words. "Love is the fundamental vibration."

"What?" Tasha's voice broke through, dispelling the memory. "I didn't quite hear that."

Opening her eyes, Bree let her gaze drift. "It's something Emily reminded me of recently." She shook her head. "My tradition teaches that all life emerges out of Love, that all life *is* Love in manifestation. And as everything is a manifestation of Love, a manifestation of the Sacred Love-Making, everything is equally Sacred."

Her eyes snapped back into focus and met Tasha's grey-blue gaze. "Masculine, Feminine, Creative—all are equally Sacred, equally Love-filled and equally Love. And since Love is the fundamental vibration, *Loving* is a sacred act—is *the* sacred act—in *all* of its manifestations."

"I agree." Tasha nodded slowly. "Bree, when you find someone you can love—whether a man or a woman—that's a Gift. For as long as it holds you, that love is a blessing."

She paused and leaned toward Bree. "You are the most devout person I know. How can you break that faith? How can you deny what the Sacred is offering you?"

Bree shifted uncomfortably in her seat. Her jeans pulled tight against her skin, pressing the stone fleur-de-lys painfully into her thigh. Rocking backward, she reached in and pulled the stone out of her pocket. She set it carefully down upon the metal table and stared.

"I'd wondered where that had gotten to."

Bree lifted her gaze. "You recognize this stone?"

"Sure. It was Gwen's." Tasha leaned back in her chair. "I have no idea where it came from, but she always carried it with her."

"She got it from me." Bree's voice rasped. "I gave it to her. A present to celebrate our first anniversary." Staring at the stone, she drew her fingers tenderly across its etched surface.

"Bree, Gwen is dead. You cannot bring her back to life. The only person you can bring to life now is you."

43

Bree walked in the dappling light streaming through the gaps in the trees of her favorite Missouri state park. Their leaf-covered branches stretched over her head, swaying ever so slightly. Her steps steady upon the large, cement paving stones, she let her gaze drift to her right, out to the muddy, racing waters of the Missouri River.

Hello, Lady. Sunlight glinted across the river's surface. Closing her eyes against the sudden glare, Bree smiled. *It's good to see you, too.*

The soft voice of the trees whispered in the breeze. Bree's black hair spilled across her cheeks and covered her eyes. She turned her face forward, into the gust, and the black strands shifted to stream behind her.

She continued along the curving walk toward the park's promontory, the meeting point of the two rivers. This deep in the woods, she could not see the Mississippi River, not yet. But the presence of the "Old Man" hummed, deep, steady and reassuring, off to her left.

Her inner awareness scanned the earth beneath her. Not for the first time she wondered if it missed being a riverbed. Whether it longed to be washed again in the constant caress of the lovemaking of the two rivers.

The path arched toward the left. As the woods fell away, Bree walked past the ancient willow tree whose limbs draped shade over a ring of educational panels. She had read them once. She knew they explained the historical connection of this confluence to the explorers Meriwether Lewis and William Clark, and their dream to see the Pacific Ocean.

She took another step and the Mississippi River shimmered into view. It stretched from her left as the Missouri flowed from her right. Bree slowed to a stop. She stood watching the two Ancients and sighed. "So beautiful."

She made her way out onto the silt-covered promontory, to the few stones brave enough to stand between the two, powerful River Spirits.

As the waters lapped closer and closer to the square toes of her boots, she reached and slid a silver flask out of her back pocket. About the size of her palm, three dragons spiraled across the flask's surface, their tails disappearing into endless, interlocking curls. Bree unscrewed the top and breathed in the peaty fragrance.

"*Uisce beatha*... The Waters of Life."

She looked into the glistening surface of the waters. "Sorry I have been away so long. I know, I should have come sooner, greeted you when I returned, but... well... I hope you can forgive me." Raising the flask up before her, she whispered, "With gratitude." Then she lowered it and emptied a pour of whiskey into each river as well as their point of confluence. "Peace be upon you. Peace be between us. And peace be."

With a brief bow, Bree stepped back from the waters. Her hair dancing with the wind, she bent over the small flask and replaced the cap before returning it to her pocket. She lifted her gaze back to the waters and a smile seeped slowly across her face.

Two figures shimmered before her. Otherworldly bright, their eyes gleamed silvery-blue in their radiant bodies. Lustrous as starlight, they glimmered and flowed, their feet disappearing into the waters of the two rivers.

They stood facing each other, their watery tresses billowing in the breeze. With a sparkling smile, the Lady of the Waters lifted her hands in welcoming before crossing the waters of the Missouri River. The Lord of the Waters reached his hands to hers and sailed across the Mississippi. Bree shivered as their fingers touched and interlaced directly over the point of confluence, the meeting point of their two rivers.

A smile, tender and inviting, flashed across the Lady's face. Ancient and ageless, the Spirit of the Missouri River drew her lover's face to hers. *"Mo ghrá... My love..."* the Spirit of the Mississippi's voice, deep and rumbling, tumbled through Bree as she watched lips welcome lips.

Bree bowed her head. "Blessed is the Mystery."

"You still don't trust me."

Bree tilted her head. Just to her right, ten mounds of pale earth appeared, side by side. Waving from left to right, the mounds rose and fell in rapid succession, and Bree's eyes tracked up the Otherworldly legs and torso of the Dagda.

The Father of the Celtic tradition shrugged. *"Not that I blame you, really. Given our history."*

Bree locked puzzled eyes with his. "What history?"

"Well," he gazed out across the flowing waters, *"your father in this lifetime, for starters. And your uncle."* He glanced at her from the corner of his eyes. *"You're not exactly close."*

That is an understatement. "No."

"Certainly no basis for trust there."

"None."

The Dagda's head bobbed slowly beside her. He picked up a stone and tossed it into the waters of the Mississippi. The stone skipped across the river's surface.

"Then we have past lives to consider. No doubt you can recall more than one lifetime in which your man left you, promising to return, then didn't."

The stone bounced off the waters of the joining rivers. Golden light flashed, igniting Bree's inner vision...

Raven-black hair falls unbound above a green woolen cloak and she draws the wool more tightly around the man before her. Blinking back tears, her eyes follow her hands as they trace the spirals she embroidered to mark his acceptance into the Mystery. With a sigh, she lifts her chin and kisses him. Without a word, she watches him board the boat and disappear across the sea.

"Phaisos, my love," her soul whispers, "come back to me."

Bree gasped. It still hurt to remember him. Her lover from a distant past, she unearthed their history during her recent visit to Scotland. He left to deepen his connection to the Sacred. And she had waited for him. Moon turning upon moon turning, she waited for Phaisos. Living each day with one eye upon the sea, she willed her love to come home to her. She begged, even pleaded with the waters to carry her love back to their bonfire. But the sea had rolled onto the shore, day after day, empty.

The stone bounced again, golden light shimmering in its leap, and Bree's vision blurred...

"Can you remember, mo Ghrá... my Love?" Bríghid's voice echoes around her. "Can you remember the heart you loved more than your own?"

Bree lowers a shaking hand onto a red-haired man's chest. In a flash, she sees it all again... his lifeless body sprawled upon the floor... her shaking hands trying to revive him... her body bent over his, pressed to his, in search of warmth but finding only cold.

"I could not save him." Her voice trembles as tears slip down her cheeks. "All my knowledge, all my training, and I could not save him."

The stone bounced a third time and whispers drifted around Bree, too low for her to hear. "Voices of the dead," she muttered into the wind. She closed her eyes and, rising from the moaning din, a voice echoed through her.

"Tha bròn orm."

Bree squeezed her eyes closed against the rising memory...

Metal pierces the man's chest and he gasps as battle-weary flesh tenses once more. His struggle sends the tear deeper until muscles rend and yield. In the falling silence, Bree hears only the wind crying through the heather as the image of a woman—tall, broad-shouldered with long, black hair whipping in the wind—turns hazel eyes upon him.

His knees buckle, returning the body to earth. "Tha bròn orm... I'm sorry..." escapes as a grunt. As his last breath casts itself to the wind, the woman closes her eyes and walks away.

Bree moaned. Fighting her way free of the howling echoes of loss after loss, she forced her eyes open. Her breath rough in her chest, she dropped her gaze to the square toes of her boots.

"I won't apologize."

Bree snapped her head up and stared at the Dagda.

He watched the stone sink into the waters. *"You needed the Mother more, then."*

"And now?"

"Now?" He tilted his head to look at her from the corners of his eyes. *"You need us both."* He lifted his right hand and gestured to the waters of the two rivers mingling before her. *"Just like this river. Beyond this point, it can reach its full potential only with the waters of both the Missouri and the Mississippi. Mother and Father uniting in Co-Creation."*

Bree stared at the flowing waters. *Truth,* her soul whispered.

"So, truce?" The Dagda's eyebrows arched. *"Can we be friends again?"*

Bree started. She turned and faced the Father of her tradition. "Again?"

His eyes twinkled and he nodded.

Again. The implications of that word threatened to knock Bree breathless. Just how deep did her soul flow?

"It would mean everything to me." He gestured to the flowing rivers. The Lord and Lady of the Waters stood watching her. *"To us. And,"* he placed his hand upon hers, *"to us."*

Bree closed her eyes and shivered.

What do I do?

"Trust, Bree Nic Bhríde," Brighid's voice rippled through her. *"Trust in Love again."*

Her heart pounding, Bree opened her eyes. The Dagda stood silhouetted by the two River Spirits. Their gleaming eyes implored her silently, *"Love, Love, Love."*

She sighed. "Friends."

44

Bree steered across the all-but-deserted highway toward the right-hand exit to interstate 170. As she merged onto the city ring road, the swollen moon gleamed overhead, illuminating her Jeep Wrangler with golden-white light.

She blinked against its brilliance and the silvery-blue light of the River Spirits' eyes swirled behind her eyelids. She went to the confluence to honor the waters, to re-establish a working relationship with them now that she had returned to the city they nourished. The visit from the Dagda had been a complete surprise.

"Can we be friends again?" The Dagda's voice echoed in her ears. *"It would mean everything to me."*

Bree frowned. *Why now? What has changed?*

Out of habit, she clicked on her blinker and merged off the highway onto Delmar Boulevard. Rolling up the exit ramp, she smiled. The light was green. *Must be my night.* She turned left and headed toward her apartment.

Golden-white moonlight shimmered across the darkened blacktop. For an instant, Chelle's bare shoulder gleamed before Bree's eyes. Smooth and silky, it peeked enticingly from under the tangerine-orange, cotton sheet.

Soft, tender kisses drifted out of Bree's memory and across her lips. *Lovely*, Bree smiled. *Truly lovely.* She glanced at her hands on the steering wheel and sighed. *But no fire.*

The traffic light ahead winked from yellow to red and Bree pressed her foot on the brake. The Jeep slowed to a stop and Bree furrowed her brow. She leaned forward to read the street sign she knew so well.

"Midland Boulevard."

She shifted her gaze to the left. The Café de Lys stared back, darkened, empty and locked for the night.

"Bree," Tasha's voice echoed within her, "when you find someone you can love—whether a man or a woman—that's a Gift. For as long as it holds you, that love is a blessing." In her inner vision, Tasha's eyes flashed before Bree. "You are the most devout person I know. How can you break that faith? How can you deny what the Sacred is offering you?"

Heat radiated through her thigh. Bree lowered her eyes and pressed her palm against the small lump in her jeans' pocket. She ran her fingers along the contours of the stone fleur-de-lys.

A car horn blared behind her and Bree jumped. She glanced up as the impatient driver sped around her. Shifting her gaze forward, she noticed the traffic light was once again green. She lifted her foot off the brake, then pressed it back down.

She twisted to her right and stared at the crossroad several feet behind her. The familiar rod-iron community gate was just visible in the brilliant moonlight. The words University Hills shimmered in the golden-white light.

"Bree, Gwen is dead." Tasha's voice rang in her ears. "You cannot bring her back to life. The only person you can bring to life now is you."

She's right.

Bree shifted forward in her seat. The traffic light at Midland Boulevard blazed green into the evening darkness. With a smile, Bree stepped on the gas pedal and continued east along Delmar Boulevard. As she passed the Gates of Opportunity, she winked at the two stone lions—one female, one male—guarding the entrance to the eclectic, entertainment district known as The Loop.

Bree sailed through green light after green light, then spotted the hulking, eight-storied, contemporary building long before its gleaming nameplate came into view. She swung the Jeep into the tiny front lot and smiled. A single, open parking spot appeared ahead of her. She pulled into the empty spot and turned off the engine.

Definitely my night.

She hopped out of the Jeep and stopped. Shifting her keys to her left hand, she reached into her right jean's pocket and pulled out the stone carving of the fleur-de-lys. With a soft sigh, she pressed the stone to her lips, then placed it gently onto the driver's seat cushion before pushing the Jeep door closed.

The double, glass doors of the Starlight Hotel slid open automatically, and Bree made her way through the blue-lit, art-deco lobby and into the empty elevator.

As she stepped into the carpeted, third-floor hallway, a deep toning reverberated around her. Her heart pounded. With each step, the deep tone pulsed with her thundering heartbeat, aching its way from her pelvis toward her heart.

305...307...309.

Bree stood facing the closed door. Her whole body vibrated. She raised her fist to knock, then hesitated.

It's late. He's probably asleep. Small black, red and white spirals spilled out of her balled hand. Bree closed her eyes. The deep, reverberating tone resounded through her heart. *Or, maybe I have lost my nerve.*

The gentle ping of an elevator chime spilled down the hall and Bree flinched. Laughter ricocheted along the walls and, a split second later, three men appeared around the corner. Cackling loudly, they headed in Bree's direction.

Her body recoiled and Bree pulled her hand away from the closed door. Shoving it into her jeans' pocket, she pressed herself close to the wall and hurried back to the elevator. As the metal doors closed in front of her, Bree leaned her head back in silence.

Now what? She stared at the elevator buttons. *Am I really prepared to leave?* Her body lurched and she pushed the button for the top floor. *Perhaps a drink in The Milky Way.*

The floors ticked by. With each chime of the elevator, small black, red and white spirals blinked to life around Bree. They swirled before her, their light throbbing in rhythm with the pinging elevator.

The doors slid open and the pulsating spirals spilled into the outdoor, rooftop bar. Without thinking, Bree followed the Otherworldly whorls past comfortable couches and colorful, art-deco tables to the open-air Observation Deck. She stopped short.

Hamish leaned against the white railing, one foot resting on the lower rung. Golden-white moonlight spilled down his broad shoulders and back, etching the edges of the fine MacLeod of Skye tartan. Bree watched the black, red and white spirals whirl around him as the deep toning resounded again through her heart.

Thank you, Great Mother. She smiled. *Blessed is the Mystery.*

Bree stepped softly closer. She reached out, slid the fingertips of her right hand down the middle of his back. Over his left shoulder, his brown eyes met hers.

Kilt swaying gently, he turned to face her.

Bree took a step closer, her eyes locked upon his face. He stood perfectly still before her, his dark eyes encouraging her.

Her hands reached for his, slid up his arms, past his shoulders to his neck. She took a step closer.

Bree's heart pounded. The deep toning flooded up her legs and pooled in her pelvis before flowing into her heart. Twining her fingers through his dark curls, she smiled, tender and loving, and drew his face to hers.

Heat seared along her skin. Her heart racing in her chest, all around her the heartbeat thundered—*Love, Love, Love.*

"*Mo ghràidh...* My love..." Hamish's voice, deep and rumbling, tumbled through Bree as her lips welcomed his.

45

Sunlight streamed through the floor-to-ceiling windows, bathing the Cafe de Lys in golden brilliance. For the third time, Bree leaned forward and adjusted the lavender throw pillows on her favorite overstuffed loveseat. Sitting back against them, she frowned. Somehow she was certain the pillows were not the problem.

"Sorry to keep you waiting." Sheila appeared from behind Bree. "A group of four arrived just as you were sitting down. But I made yours last, so it's hot." She bent forward and placed the steaming mug upon the table in front of Bree. "Americano, black, no sugar."

"Thanks, Sheila." Bree shifted forward in her seat and picked up the white, ceramic mug. "You are fabulous."

A smile beamed across Sheila's face. She shrugged her left shoulder, tossing her red curls. "Anytime."

The front door opened, swirling golden motes of sunlight through the café. Bree glanced up at the new arrival and stared into familiar green eyes. She forced herself to swallow the coffee in her mouth and set her mug on the table. As Chelle approached, Bree clenched her hands nervously and rose from the loveseat.

Chelle's genuine smile greeted her. "Sorry I'm late."

"Not very. Besides," Bree stretched open her hands and gestured to her left, "Sheila has been keeping me company." She turned to offer the red-haired barista a smile and stopped short. Sheila stood, arms crossed tight against her chest, glaring at the new arrival.

"Hello, Sheila." Chelle's voice was welcoming. "Nice to meet you. And thanks for looking after Bree."

Sheila's eyes narrowed.

Bree spoke into the thorny silence. "Chelle, what would you like to drink?"

"Nothing, thanks."

"You're sure?"

Chelle chuckled. "Very."

Bree smiled and glanced at Sheila. "I guess you're off the hook, then."

Sheila stood stone still, glowering at Chelle. Just as Bree thought she would need to remind the barista not to be rude, Sheila slowly unfolded her arms and walked away.

Chelle shook her head. "I really can't stay long."

"Well, thanks for coming." Bree gestured to the seat beside her. "I owe you an apology. I should have said goodbye in person the other morning."

Chelle leaned sideways in the loveseat and draped an arm over the back of the chair. "No worries, hon. I'm a late sleeper and, to be honest, I was grateful for the rest. Besides, I should be apologizing to you. I should have told you about Zhenia." She grimaced. "I didn't know she was coming back to town."

"You two are..." Bree's eyebrows pulsed, "...together?"

Chelle nodded. "Zhenia's an interpreter and she spends most of her time abroad on assignment. Years ago we agreed—the only way to make it work between us is to have an open relationship." Chelle shrugged. "When she is away, we are both free to see whomever we please. But when she comes home, we are together. A couple." She sighed. "Some people find it strange, but... it works for us." She leaned forward and rested her hand on Bree's knee. "I would have explained it to you if we ever got together again."

Bree gazed into Chelle's green eyes. "Actually," she smiled, "I'm glad I didn't know."

"Are you upset?"

"No." Bree shook her head. "But I might have acted differently had I known. And I am grateful I didn't." She ran her hand down Chelle's cheek. "We've had this coming for a long time."

"I suppose we did." Chelle reached up, took Bree's hand into hers and kissed it softly.

Bree squeezed the woman's hand. "I'm glad it was you."

"Friends?"

"Always."

Chelle tilted her head. "You are so good to me."

"Nothing easier, hon."

Bree leaned forward and slid her arms around Chelle's shoulders. With a smile, she drew Chelle close. As their embrace released, green eyes hovered before her and Chelle's lips pressed, soft and tender, against Bree's.

"I should go." Chelle rose to standing, then hesitated. "See you at the pub?"

Bree lifted her gaze to Chelle's and nodded. "You can count on it."

"Good."

Bree watched Chelle's swaying form weave its way across the café. As the cropped and red-tipped, brown hair disappeared out the front door, Bree pressed her right fingertips to her lips.

So lovely. But no fire.

She chuckled. Dropping her hand into her lap, she shifted forward and reached for her coffee.

Sunlight glinted off red curls and Bree's heart fluttered. *Gwen?* Her head snapped toward the rosy light. Cold, brown eyes met her gaze.

Bree's cheek stung, as if she had been slapped, and she furrowed her brow. "Everything okay, Sheila?"

Without a word, the red-headed barista spun on her heel and stalked away.

46

"*Bree...*" A woman's soft burr echoed through Bree's awareness.

Bree's eyes fluttered behind closed lids. Her consciousness floating slowly up and out of the formless depths of sleep, she sighed. "Mmmmmm?"

She drifted. Her dreaming self strained to hear whatever had called her from the world of dreams. But only a vast thrumming, deep and broad, like the hum of bees within a hive, greeted her.

Female. Bree's brow creased. *Female what?*

The murmuring hum swelled louder.

Bree rolled onto her back and her arms uncurled themselves. As they stretched to her sides, a cool draft spilled over her neck and shoulders, and Bree opened her eyes.

The wooden blades of her bedroom ceiling fan stretched above her.

She pulled the sage green comforter back up and dropped her head to the right. Dark curls spilled across the white pillow case next to hers. With a smile, she rolled onto her right side and snuggled against Hamish's sleeping body. Her head tucked along his shoulder, she closed her eyes.

"*Bree...*"

Bree's eyes popped open. Her body utterly still, her eyes scanned the room around her but found nothing.

She rolled onto her back, listening intently. She was awake now and certain—someone had called her name.

"Bree..."

The familiar woman's voice rumbled in her left ear and, this time, Bree smiled.

Caitlin.

She glanced back at Hamish, still sleeping beside her. She kissed his shoulder softly, then rolled gently out of the bed. Stepping into her closet, she pulled a pair of jeans off a nearby hanger and slid into them. Then she grabbed a favorite shirt. She was still fastening the buttons as she tip-toed out the bedroom, closed the door behind her and padded quietly up the hall.

In the living room, she picked up her telephone from the bookshelf that had become its overnight home. Unplugging the power cord, she woke it out of sleep mode and frowned.

No new messages.

Lifting her chin, she gazed past the open blinds and out the window at the oak leaves glinting in the moonlight.

I definitely heard Caitlin.

With a nod, Bree turned and walked across the living room. She scrolled through her list of contacts, pulled up her kinswoman's number and pressed dial. The tell-tale, European double ring sounded in her ear as she settled herself onto the loveseat.

"Bree?" Caitlin's brogue spilled from the telephone as the line connected. "I was just thinking about ye."

"I know," Bree smiled. "I heard you."

Her friend chuckled, then fell quiet. "Are ye angry with me?"

Bree frowned. "For what?"

"For Hamish."

Bree rose from the loveseat. Stepping into the center of the living room, she glanced down the hall to her bedroom door. "No," her voice flowed soft and warm, "not at all."

"He found ye then?"

"He did. And I am grateful."

Through the window, Bree watched the silvery-white moonlight dance along the edges of the swaying oak leaves. Her vision blurred and the leaves flowed into the rippling waters of Loch Dunvegan. For a heartbeat, she was back in Heather House, staring out the big, bay window of the inn's cozy den. As her living room reappeared around her, Bree inhaled.

"Caitlìn, I was thinking. If you could use an extra pair of hands around Heather House, for any reason, please let me know. I... I'd be happy to come and help for a while."

"I've told ye before," her kinswoman's soft burr washed over Bree, "ye have a place here any time ye have need or want of it."

47

Bree steered her Jeep Wrangler along the winding drive of the Sophia Center. Smiling through the dappling light at the ancient trees along the lane, she followed the final curve into the parking lot behind the center. The soft voice of the trees rustled around her as she pulled the truck into her usual parking space.

"Welcome back, Bree Nic Bhríde," the willow tree before her swayed.

"Thanks." She bowed her head in greeting. "It's good to be here."

It really is, this time. She cut the engine and leaned back against the seat. *Blessed is the Mystery.*

The bouncing notes of an Irish jig filled the Jeep. She pulled her vibrating telephone out of her jeans' pocket and glanced at it. Fergus' number glowed on the screen. A grin stretching the corner of her mouth, she pressed answer and lifted the telephone to her ear.

"You playing hookey from the clinic today?"

Fergus' soft chuckle drifted around her. "No. Just in between patients and thought I would give you a call. In fact, I have a message for you."

"From whom?"

"Pamela."

Bree inhaled slowly. She glanced at the open cup holder beside her. Gwen's stone fleur-de-lys still rested there. Bree prodded it with her finger and waited, but the stone remained whole and intact. She exhaled. "How is she?"

"Very well. She and Kat had a long talk after your last session with them. They have decided to stop their attempts to conceive. She said you would understand."

Bree said nothing.

"She also asked me to say... thank you."

And thank you, Great Goddess, Mother Brighid and all my Allies. Bree smiled. "Glad we could help."

"Bree, you more than help. You care. I know it, and so do Kat and Pamela."

Silence drifted between them.

"Listen... I don't mean to push, really. But..." Fergus sighed. Bree could sense his hesitation. She gripped the steering wheel with her free hand and closed her eyes. "I was thinking... If you are planning to stay in town for a while, you are welcome to use the extra room in my clinic."

Bree's eyes popped open.

"I know," he rushed forward, tripping over his words, "you would probably prefer to be back in Jess' office. But, the space really is perfect for you and your work, and I can't think of anyone I would prefer to have in my office." He paused. "That is, presuming you are planning to start seeing clients again."

Bree exhaled slowly.

"Look," Fiery red hair flashed through Bree's inner vision, "don't answer now. But, do me a favor and think about it? Please?"

Bree chuckled. "When you put it that way... Of course. I'll consider it."

"Good." He paused. "You can still have a life here, Bree, if you want it."

The line disconnected and Bree stared at the blank screen of her telephone.

"He loves you."

Bree glanced toward the passenger seat and Gwen's ghostly image returned her gaze. Bree nodded. "I know."

With a sigh, Bree pushed open the door and slid out of the Jeep.

Gravel rumbling beneath her square-toed boots, she crossed the parking lot to the edge of the park itself and hesitated. Her left foot hovered, suspended over the grassy earth of the woodland. *Am I sure?* She set her foot down again. *Will I even be welcome?*

The wooden archway caught her gaze. Just beyond that woven trellis, silvery-blue light shimmered and swirled as the Lady of the Labyrinth reached flowing arms out to Bree.

Blessings, Lady. Bree bowed her head. *What Truth would you speak to me today?*

Opalescent light flashed and Bree lifted her gaze.

"*Come, Raven Child.*" The Lady of the Labyrinth smiled. "*Come, step into my circle and let me whisper It into your heart.*"

Thank you. Bree rested her left hand upon her heart. *Blessed is the Mystery.*

Bree lifted her foot and stepped onto the open field.

Grass dancing around her ankles, she worked her way across the rolling earth of the Center's wild meadow. A deep, sweetness permeated the air and she glanced to her left. Small, pink blossoms dotted her favorite ring of apple trees.

"*Remember to pick some for me this season.*"

Bree's head swung to her right. Gwen's ghostly form walked silently beside her, the grass undisturbed under her favorite, red, Danish clogs.

The woven trellis marking the entrance to the labyrinth drifted steadily closer and Bree slowed to a stop beside it. She stared at the familiar archway in silence, then faced Gwen.

"One more walk together?"

Sorrow filled her former lover's eyes. Silently, Gwen shook her head and peered over her left shoulder.

An enormous, silver-white door opened behind Gwen. Bree stared at the brilliant, white light spilling from the ever-widening opening. Without moving, she watched it flow steadily and intently toward her former lover.

Gwen lifted her arms in welcome.

Opalescent light flashed and Bree blinked against the brilliance. As Bree's vision resolved, white light suffused Gwen's ghostly form. Her energetic field shimmered while the edges of her soul form slowly seeped through the door and into the Otherworld.

"It's time I was going."

"I was surprised you stayed so long."

Gwen tilted her head and her fading form blanched. *"I needed to know you would be okay."*

Bree nodded.

Light streaming from her eyes, Gwen glanced at Bree. Something heavy and solid pulled against her jeans and Bree reached into her bulging, front pocket. The stone fleur-de-lys fell into her hand. Frowning slightly, she met Gwen's radiant gaze.

"Place it under the tree at the center of the labyrinth for me?"

Bree blinked back tears. "Of course."

The soft sigh of silver bells spilled through the open door and rippled Gwen's transparent form. Gleaming, she kissed her hand and blew the kiss to Bree. Her soul form rippled with her breath and shook off all remaining constraint. Pure, free, blazing Light, Gwen's soul flowed with the chimes through the door and into the Otherworld.

"Goodbye." Bree kissed her empty hand and blew the kiss through the closing door. "May the Goddess welcome you Home."

Before her, the midday sky stretched calm and cloudless, the Otherworldly door vanished into that cerulean gleam. Bree looked around her. For a moment, she wondered if it had been there at all.

She looked down at her right hand. The stone fleur-de-lys pressed against her skin and she sighed.

Blessed is the Mystery.

Closing her fingers around the stone, she turned to her left. The wooden trellis was there. Beyond it, the labyrinth waited for her.

"Come, Raven Child." The Lady of the Labyrinth called. *"Come, step into my circle and let me whisper Truth into your heart."*

Bree inhaled slowly and stepped into the labyrinth.

48

Bree lifted the empty suitcase over her head and slid it onto the closet shelf. Eyes trained on the black fabric, she stepped back and propped her hands on her hips. "Have a good rest, but don't get too comfortable," she nodded. "I might need you again... very soon."

Chuckling softly to herself, she switched off the closet light and stepped out into the bedroom. She pushed the open drawer of her dresser closed and headed into the hall. Wool socks slipping on the oakwood floor, she padded past the kitchen and guest room.

She could just see her Café de Lys mug resting on the dining room table. The tea it contained was, no doubt, cold. She had poured it after returning from her walk that morning at the labyrinth. What had propelled her out of the chair and into her room to unpack, she still did not know. She had left the cup behind without a second thought. Now it gleamed in the afternoon sun, a brilliant white beside the deep red of Hamish's roses.

"*Mo ghràidh...* My love..." Hamish's deep burr rumbled through Bree. Her skin blazed with the memory of his lips, soft and warm upon her, and she sighed.

The crimson petals held her gaze as she crossed in front of the dining room table. Without thinking, she slowed and let her fingers drift along their tender edges.

She stepped into the living room and the deep groan of metal shifting echoed through the room. Bree turned to see the front door swing open, revealing Hamish's broad shoulders. She pressed her lips together to stifle a smile.

"The intrepid explorer returns!"

Hamish glanced up at her, his dark eyes stormy.

"So," she forced a rising laugh back down her throat and settled onto the loveseat. "How was the Arch?"

Kilt thrashing his knees, he stalked into the living room. "Ye could hae warned me!"

Bree willed herself not to laugh. "Warned you? About what, exactly?"

"Och, aye," Hamish moaned, "ye know right and well about what." He pitched his voice high, mimicking the cadence of her own. "I dinnae need to go again, Hamish. I've been so many times, Hamish." He glared at her. "Ye minx. Ye did nae wanna climb intae thae wee excuses for lifts!"

Despite herself, Bree laughed out loud.

"Tha's right, you laugh! But t'was I had tae sit, my knees up tae my oysters, wi' four strangers in a pod no bigger than an egg!" He grabbed his kilt and pulled the edges close around him. "I kep fearin' they could see me..." he stammered silently, his face slowly turning crimson, "...and all!"

The flush seeped down her lover's neck as he struggled to collapse his broad form into something small.

Bree's vision shimmered and cleared, and before her eyes an equally crimson Hamish hunched awkwardly, crammed into the middle seat of the tiny tram capsule. Surrounded by four complete strangers—and desperately clutching his kilt to his skin—he stared miserably at the one and only, miniscule window in the center of the tram door. Then, the whole image tilted on its side, only to right itself again and again, like a manually-adjusted ferris-wheel chair.

Bree pressed her lips together. Fighting to preserve his Highland dignity, she reminded herself just how close to an eternity the four minutes from the visitor center to the observation deck at the top of the arch, three hundred and seventy-two feet above the ground, could seem. But the Otherworldly vision of Hamish rolled onto its side once again, and she chortled loudly.

Hamish's mouth gaped. "Have ye no mercy?"

Bree's body shook. Unable to restrain herself, she closed her eyes, collapsed onto her side, and roared.

"Tis no laughing matter!"

Bree opened her eyes. Hands on his hips and eyes glowering, Hamish stood before her. The image of him in the tiny pod-like tram flashed anew, and she lost herself to the rising tide.

"Stop." Hamish took a step toward her. His kilt swayed along the left edge of her field of view, and Bree fought back a snort. "I mean it... Ye'd be wise tae settle down now... If ye dunnae stop laughing..."

She could not help herself. Rolling her head along the cushion of the loveseat, Bree reached up and wiped away the tears spilling from her eyes.

"Right. Tha's it!"

Hamish marched toward her. Strong hands pinned her down, then tickled the sides of her torso.

Bree writhed. "Stop it!"

"Och, aye!" He grinned over her. "Now ye find your tongue!"

"Hamish!"

"Mmmmmmm?" His deep laugh rumbled beside her ear.

Extricating her left hand from the frenzy, she reached up, slid her fingers through his dark curls, and pulled his lips to hers.

EPILOGUE

Bree MacLeod stood wrapped in the mist-filled quiet of the Kildare countryside. Her square-toed boots slowly sinking into the rain-soaked earth of Bríghid's sacred enclosure, she lifted her gaze and considered the brooding sky overhead. She had spent enough time on Éireann's Isle to know those low-hanging clouds promised another thorough soaking, and soon.

The early-November breeze nipped down her face, chilling her neck and tossing dark hair across her eyes. Turning into the gust to clear her view, she stuffed her bare hands into the pockets of her favorite black, fleece jacket and hugged it more tightly around her.

Should have made Fiona wear that scarf.

Bree's eyes drifted to the small form of her niece, hunkered precariously upon the two, narrow, moss-covered, stone steps leading down to the waters of Bríghid's sacred spring. Long, red hair spilled down the girl's shoulders to hover just above the waters' edge.

For a moment, flowing hands seemed to reach up and drag Fiona by the hair down into their watery abode. Bree started toward the girl, her arms already reaching to pull her niece to safety. But, before Bree even lifted her foot, the vision was gone. Instead, Fiona rose from her place beside the pool and walked toward Bree.

She stepped closer to her niece. "Are you cold?"

Somber, hazel eyes averted Bree's. The girl shook her head once, then stared at the soggy ground.

Something pushed against her, slowing her advance, and Bree stopped short. The energetic rebuff rolled over her, and she paused. *Did that come from Fiona?* Bree hesitated, then gestured to the willow seat, damp but available at the edge of the enclosure. "Would you like to sit?"

Fiona glanced at the stone bench beneath the twined willow branches. Her body tensed as her furtive gaze traced the enclosure from north, to east, to south, to west and back again, before offering Bree a single, curt nod.

Walking alongside her niece in silence, Bree considered the girl. Gone was the cheerful, easy-natured child of their last encounter almost two years ago. This Fiona was far too serious to turn circles wildly in her mother's kitchen or anywhere else. And the flaming red hair that had danced Bree into the Otherworld now hung limp and lackluster down the girl's back.

What has happened? Bree slid her chilled hands back into her jacket pockets. *Mother Bríghid, show me the way. Guide me to the healing question.*

Her exhale billowing as mist before her, Bree's training engaged. She peered past the dark smudges encircling the girl's eyes and the slack, almost sickly pallor of Fiona's face. Softening her gaze, Bree looked with her Otherworldly eyes at the energetic field surrounding her niece. The image of a locked, leaden door flashed through her inner vision.

Fiona flinched. Stopping dead in her tracks, the girl turned fierce, wild eyes upon Bree.

An undeniable, energetic slap stung across Bree's cheeks. As she blinked back tears, her cousine Rose's voice echoed through her awareness.

"Something is very wrong with Fiona."

GLOSSARY

IRISH, SCOTS GAELIC, AND RUSSIAN PHRASES AND
PRONUNCIATION

The sounds of the English language differ from those of the Irish, Scots Gaelic and Russian. The pronunciations listed here are attempts at phonetic renderings of Gaelic and Russian sounds. Please know that these are approximations only, a starting point for those daring enough to try.

A stór... dearest, my dear, darling. Used to refer to a cherished family member or loved one. Pronounced "uh store."

Ach... Both Irish and Scots Gaelic, literally "But" or "Well". Pronounced "ach" with the ch aspirated in the throat (like the word "loch").

Aes Dána... the Gifted, those blessed by the goddess Dánu / Dána and imbued with Otherworldly skills. Pronounced "ace donna."

Airds... the directions of the Celtic Wheel: north, east, south, west and center. Pronounced like "arts" but with "air" in place of "ar"... "air-ts."

Alba... in Irish and Scots Gaelic, this is the word for Scotland. Pronounced "all-buh."

Anam cara... soul friends. Pronounced "on-um car-uh."

Bean Feasa... wise woman, shaman, walker between the worlds. Pronounced "bahn fah-sah."

Beannachtaí... blessings. Pronounced "bahn-nach-tee," with the "nach" aspirated in the throat.

Beannachtaí, a stór... Blessings, dearest. Pronounced "bahn-nach-tee a store."

Beannachtaí, mo Ghrá... Blessings, my love. Pronounced "bahn-nach-tee moe hraw."

Bean-Sìdhe... A woman of the Ancient Ones, a banshee. Pronounced "Bahn-she."

Bodhrán... the Irish word for a traditional, round, Irish, wooden frame drum. Pronounced "bow-rawn."

Bree Nic Bhríde... Bree MacLeod's Gaelic name, literally meaning Bree daughter of Bríde. Pronounced "bree nick vree-je."

Bríde... a variation of the name Bríghid. Pronounced "bree-je."

Brígh... a variation of the name Bríghid. Pronounced "bree-he," with the "he" as a slight aspiration in the throat at the end.

Bríghid... the Celtic goddess of the forge, smithcraft, poetry, midwifing and the keeper of the Sacred Flame. Pronounced "bree-hid" or "bree-git."

Brónagh... Irish woman's name, means sad or sorrowful. Pronounced "bro-nuh" ("bro" as in the shortened version of "brother").

Caitlìn... Irish and Scottish woman's name, a version of Kathleen. Pronounced "kuh-shleen."

Chiya... although not actually Irish, the word deserves explanation. First encountered in Marion Zimmer Bradley's *Darkover* series, the term has stayed in my vocabulary. The closest translation is *dearest*, *dear heart* or *beloved*. Pronounced "chee-yuh" or "shee-yuh."

Cill Dara... Irish for Kildare, a town in Leinster, Ireland, associated with the goddess Brighid.

Clouties... strips of cloth or ribbon tied to sacred trees in a Celtic act of prayer. Like prayer ties, they are left on special trees to carry the prayer to the Sacred through the elements. (Also spelled *clooties*.)

Deiseal...Irish for sunwise or clockwise movement. To turn *deiseal* is to invoke the positive, constructive flow of creation. Pronounced "Jay-shull."

Éireann... Ireland. Also the name of one of the three mother goddesses of Ireland. Pronounced "erin."

Ériu... The mother goddess of Ireland. Also written Éire or Érin. Pronounced "air-ree-uh."

Fáilte abhaile... Welcome home. Pronounced "fall-chuh a-wall-ye."

Fáth Fíth... an incantation chanted to cast a cloak of invisibility upon someone. Pronounced "faw fee."

Fiona... an Irish girl's name, meaning "Bright" or "Fair one". Pronounced "fee-oh-na."

Go raibh mille maith agaibh... Thank you (formal or form multiple people). Pronounced "go rev meal-uh my uh-give."

Go raibh mille maith agat... Thank you (singular, for one person). Pronounced "go rev meal-uh my uh-gut."

Is deas bualadh leat... Lovely to meet you. Pronounced "iss jass bull-uh lot."

Imbas... The light of illumination and inspiration that flows at the heart of all creation and creative activity. Pronounced like the English word "emboss," only with equal stress upon both syllables, "im-boss."

Long mór... The Dagda's club of death and healing. Also called the *long anfaid* in Irish, one end of the club renders death to those touched, while the other restores life.

Machair... the soil, the earth of Ireland. Pronounced "ma-hair."

Manannán mac Lir... The Irish god of the sea and the underwater realms. A master of magic and wisdom, he owns many magical items, including the Cup of Truth, a silver branch and a crane bag of healing items. Pronounced "Maw-nah-noun mock leer."

Mo Ghrá... my love. Pronounced "moe hraw."

Mo ghràidh... Scots Gaelic for "My love." Pronounced "moe hraw."

Ní hea... literally in Irish, "It isn't." Used colloquially and here as "no." Pronounced "knee-hah."

Pàiste an Shìdhe... Scots Gaelic for "Child of the People of Peace." Pronounced "paw-sh-tuh on ee-yuh."

Poidiomte... in Russian, literally "Let's go" or "Let's get out of here." Pronounced "paw-ee-jome-chuh."

Sasannach... in both Irish and Scots Gaelic, literally "Englishman" or "person from England." Colloquially used to mean interloper, intruder or one who does not belong. Pronounced "suh-sen-ach."

Scotia... The Mother Goddess of Scotland, after whom Scotland and Nova Scotia are named. Pronounced "skoh-shuh."

Skean dubh... Scots Gaelic, the name of a small, single-edged knife traditionally kept concealed in the legging or boot. Pronounced "skee-un doov."

the Sídhe... also called the People of Peace and the Ancient Ones. The *Sídhe* are the ancient guardians of and the in dwelling spirits of the land. *Sídhe* is pronounced "she."

Sin é... literally, "It is". Used as the equivalent of "Amen" or "So mote it be". Pronounced "shin-a," with the "a" sounding long, as in "hay," but without the "h" sound.

Síocháin daoibh... Irish for "Peace be upon you." Pronounced "she-uh-hawn yee-vuh."

Síocháin duit... Irish for "Peace be upon you." Pronounced "she-uh-hawn doot."

Tapadh leat... Scots Gaelic for "Thank you." Used for single individual. Pronounced "tuh-pug lot."

Tapadh libh... Also Scots Gaelic for "Thank you." Used for multiple people or when speaking respectfully. Pronounced "tuh-pug live."

Thà bròn orm... Scots Gaelic for "I am sorry." Pronounced "haw brone or-um."

Tha e gu bòidheach... Scots Gaelic for "That is beautiful" or "It is beautiful." Pronounced "haw eh guh baw-nuch," with the ch aspirated in the throat (like the word "loch").

Thà fàilte romhat... Scots Gaelic for "You are welcome." Pronounced "haw fall-chuh row-ut."

Tricele... Sometimes called a triskele or triskelion. A Tricele is an ancient (Neolithic) image comprised of three conjoined spiraling lines that meet in the center.

Uisce beatha... literally, "Waters of life." The Irish word for whiskey. Pronounced "ish-kuh bay-huh."

Vse khorosho... Russian for "Is everything okay?" Pronounced "fs-yo huh-ruh-show."

REFERENCES & RESOURCES

For those curious souls who would like to know more about the Otherworld, Celtic mysticism, the shamanic universe and the concepts presented in this book, here are some doorways:

Berresford Ellis, Peter. *Celtic Myths and Legends.* Running Press, 1999.

Carr-Gomm, Philip. *Druid Mysteries.* Rider, 2002.

Carr-Gomm, Philip and Stephanie. *The Druid Animal Oracle.* Simon & Schuster, 1994.

Cowan, Tom. *Fire in the Head.* Harper San Francisco, 1993.

Cowan, Tom. *Shamanism as a Spiritual Practice.* The Crossing Press, 1996.

Eisler, Riane. *The Chalice and the Blade.* Harper Collins, 1988.

Eliade, Mircea. *Shamanism.* Princeton University Press, 1964.

Greer, John Michael. *The Druid Handbook*. Red Wheel/Weiser, LLC, 2006.

Greer, John Michael. *The Sacred Geometry Oracle*. Llewellyn Publications, 2002.

Hamilton, Claire. *Maiden, Mother, Crone*. O Books, 2005.

Hughes, Kristoffer. *From the Cauldron Born*. Llewellyn Publications, 2012.

Huntley, H.E. *The Divine Proportion*. Dover Publications, Inc., 1970.

Lundy, Miranda. *Sacred Geometry*. Walker & Company, 2001.

Maciocia, Giovanni. *The Foundations of Chinese Medicine*. Churchill Livingstone, 1989.

Matthews, Caitlín. *Singing the Soul Back Home*. Element Books Limited, 1995.

Matthews, John. *The Celtic Shaman: A Handbook*. Element Books, 1991.

Matthews, John. *Healing the Wounded King*. Element Books, 1997.

Mitchell, Stephen. *The Second Book of the Tao*. Penguin Books, 2009.

Mitchell, Stephen. *Tao Te Ching*. Harper Perennial, 1991.

Pennick, Nigel. *The Sacred World of the Celts*. Inner Traditions International, 1997.

Restall Orr, Emma. *Living Druidry*. Piatkus, 2004.

Sills, Franklyn. *The Polarity Process*. Element Books, 1989.

ACKNOWLEDGMENTS

This third journey into Bree MacLeod's story carried me into unexpected twists and turns. For all those brave souls who supported me and my Highest Good, both in This World and the Otherworld, through the various stages of that process... thank you.

Go raibh mille maith agaibh... thank you Goddess, God, Creator, for Your endless patience, guidance and unswerving Love. Goddess Bríghid, Raven, and my Council of Allies, thank You for singing back to me the song of my soul, even when I could not recognize it.

Great Goddess, may Your children find within this story a pathway back to Your sacred song.

As always, I am incredibly grateful for my Critique Group partners: Brad R. Cook, Cole Gibsen and TW Fendley. Your words and silences continue to make me a better author. And the (Un)Stable Writers, Ben Moeller-Gaa, Jess Moeller-Gaa and Autumn Rinaldi, thank you for illuminating the hidden treasures within these pages.

Heartfelt thanks to my fantastic advance copy readers: Faye Schrater, James Wood and Pam DeVoe. We got there in the end.

I continue to be blessed to work with Stefanie Stearns, the best editor ever. I am so grateful for you.

This book would not be complete without the stunning cover art that enfolds it. Lesley Lenox, thank you for your creative vision, patience, and dedication to getting it right. Speaking of images, my remarkable photographer, Ted Moreno, deserves to take a bow. Thank you for sharing your unique ability to capture the dance of Dark, Light and Mystery.

Diolch yn fawr to my *anam cara*, fellow druid and shamanic soul walker, James Wood. Your care and support sheltered me through the end of this wild ride. You are a Gift.

And thanks, thanks and more thanks to all you wonderful readers who begged for more of Bree MacLeod's story. Your patience is finally rewarded! Enjoy *The Chalice and the Blade*. Hopefully, book four, *Thresholds*, will be finished in time for next February.

Beannachtaí... Blessings.
Jennifer Lynn

ABOUT THE AUTHOR

Jennifer Lynn is a soul midwife, a shamanic Druid Priestess, and a modern-day mystic specializing in Celtic mystical techniques and practices. During twenty-plus years of training and experience, she has studied extensively with Tom Cowan, Caitlín Matthews, Geo Cameron, the Invisible Druid Order, the Order of Bards Ovates and Druids, the Foundation for Shamanic Studies as well as with mystical practitioners internationally.

An award-winning, published poet, Jennifer gives voice to her Bardic craft through poetry and prose. She is the author of the mystical fiction series Bree MacLeod's Story. Her writings explore the rhythms of life while honoring the Goddess and the Sacred Conversation.

Jennifer is also a Chinese medicine practitioner and a Minister of the Circle of the Sacred Earth, a church of animism fostering shamanic principles and practices.

For more about Jennifer Lynn and to follow Bree MacLeod's Story, visit:

www.ThroughShamansEyes.wordpress.com.

ALSO BY JENNIFER LYNN

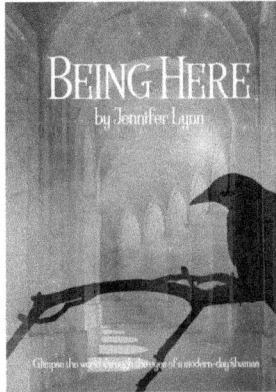

Being Here, book one of Bree MacLeod's Story

Coming Home, book two of Bree MacLeod's Story

Coming in 2021... *Thresholds,* book four of

Bree MacLeod's Story

Milton Keynes UK
Ingram Content Group UK Ltd.
UKHW021451200824
1326UKWH00045B/574

9 780999 843413